Ana Kim began her writing journey with fantastical stories about vampires and werewolves discovering their abilities and fighting against old lords from another country. After attending writing classes and finding the courage to share her tales with others, she discovered her love for thriller and adult romance. Ana's works have since transformed, focusing on gay characters and their journeys told through different genres.

To my family, for always believing in me and supporting me through my journeys in life. I love you all.

And to Vincent Cheng for asking me to write you a story and giving me the inspiration to do so. If it weren't for you, Luke and Jack wouldn't exist.

Ana Kim

LOVE HURTS

AUSTIN MACAULEY PUBLISHERS™

LONDON • CAMBRIDGE • NEW YORK • SHARJAH

Ordering Information
Quantity sales: Special discounts are available on quantity purchases by corporations, associations, and others. For details, contact the publisher at the address below.

Publisher's Cataloging-in-Publication data
Kim, Ana
Love Hurts

ISBN 9798886932713 (Paperback)
ISBN 9798886932720 (ePub e-book)

Library of Congress Control Number: 2023918568

www.austinmacauley.com/us

First Published 2024
Austin Macauley Publishers LLC
40 Wall Street, 33rd Floor, Suite 3302
New York, NY 10005
USA

mail-usa@austinmacauley.com
+1 (646) 5125767

Thank you to the editorial board for seeing the potential in
my story and to all who helped along the way.

Part 1

6:45

"Luke, sweetie, it's time for school." Luke heard his maid Patricia call out from across the room. She opened the curtains and he groaned. It was another weekday at the Finnegan residence.

"Morning, Patricia," Luke mumbled, rubbing his eyes before getting up and heading to the bathroom. She smiled and stepped aside. "I will lay your uniform out for you." Luke nodded and closed the door, undressing. Aside from the breakfast the chefs would cook him, Luke's favorite part of his morning were his baths. They were always at the right temperature and let him drown in his thoughts until it was time to go. He got into the water, sinking his entire body under it. He slowly came back up and slicked his blonde hair back, looking over at the body length mirror on the wall by the sink. Luke pulled his hair back so often, he barely needed gel anymore. He looked back down at the water and shook his head, letting the gold strands fall into his face. When he looked back up, he couldn't help but laugh. His girlfriend would hate his hair like this. Luke sighed and sunk back down until the tip of his nose barely touched the water. He took a few breaths and closed his eyes.

"Luke, you're going to be late." He suddenly heard, his eyes shooting open. He looked over at the clock above the bathroom door and huffed. It always felt like he'd close his eyes for a second and time would move so quickly. He got out of the bath, wrapping the plush towel laid out on the bathroom counter for him around his waist and walked out of the room. Luke walked over to his bed and began putting on his dark-blue uniform.

After he was fully dressed, he headed downstairs, book bag in hand. He walked into the dining room and saw a half empty glass of orange juice, a mug with coffee stains, and plates smeared with egg yolk. His parents had already left for work. Luke grabbed a piece of toast and took a bite.

"Are you not going to eat breakfast?" Patricia suddenly asked, startling him. He looked at the large, oak table again and shook his head. His least favorite part of the morning? Sitting all alone at the dining table hearing the clinking of his silverware against his plate.

"Toast will do," Luke reassured. Patricia only nodded and Luke smiled at her before heading outside. A limo pulled up and the passenger window lowered.

"Good morning, Luke," the driver greeted, waving at him. Luke jogged down the large concrete steps of his house and got into the car.

"Morning, Ralph," he sighed. Ralph had been with the family way before Luke was even born. And just like Patricia, he seemed to be around more than Luke's parents. Luke took another bite of his toast and stared out the window.

You look so perfect standing there, in my American Apparel underwear-

As the alarm rang, Jack searched for his phone, slapping his hand against his end table and feeling the buzzing against his fingertips. He grabbed it and turned it off. He groaned, still holding his phone in his hand.

"Alright, buddy," he muttered to himself, his eyes closed. "Time to get up." He counted to three in his head, but his body didn't move. Jack groaned again, forced his body up, and looked at his phone.

7:45

"Shit!" he grumbled, tossing his covers to the side. His foot got stuck and he wiggled it free before standing. How many times did he press snooze? "Shit." Jack put his phone back on the end table and sped-walk to the small bathroom down the hall. One shower and two rows of brushed teeth later, and he was headed back to his room to get dressed.

"Did you just wake up, kiddo?" Jack looked over to his bedroom door and nodded at his father.

"Yeah. I must've pressed snooze," he replied, pulling a white, wrinkled button up out of his drawer.

"Do you need a ride?" Jack looked at his father. His eyes were low, and the bags under them hung even lower. He always offered to drive him to school, even if he was still lying in bed, half awake. Jack began searching for the rest of his uniform and shook his head.

"It's okay, Dad. I'll take my skateboard."

"You sure? I can—"

"It's okay," Jack interrupted. He looked at his father again and reassured, "I take it all the time. Plus, you got off pretty late this morning." His father smiled and sighed.

"Have a good day, kiddo." Jack smiled back before he finished getting ready.

Once his shoes were on, he headed downstairs and into the kitchen. He grabbed a granola bar, water, and made his way to the front door.

Luke jogged up the steps of Thomas Pry, making his way to his classroom on the second floor.

"Hi, Luke," a girl called out to him. He smiled at her and she quickly turned to her friend to tell her the exciting news.

"Hey, Luke," another greeted. Luke waved at her, continuing up the steps.

"Luke, you're winning that match tonight, right?" a guy asked. They shared a handshake and Luke chuckled.

"For sure," he replied. After he joined the fencing team, a couple years ago, it seemed to gain him some popularity. When he reached his classroom, he walked in and sat in his usual seat, two rows back and to the right.

"Hey, baby," Luke turned to the girl beside him and smirked. It was Trish, his girlfriend of almost half a year. She kissed him on the cheek, and he returned the favor, but caught her lips instead.

"Hey," Luke said, smiling. "You coming over later?"

"Only if you win tonight's match." Luke scowled at Trish and she bit her lip, her long, black curls swinging as she turned away.

Jack stepped off his skateboard, picked it up and walked into the school building. As he made his way to his locker, he was quickly reminded why he snoozed his alarm. It was his second week here, but people still stared at him. So what if he didn't have a maid, or his own car, or crazy rich parents? He excelled in his classes and received offers from reputable universities. Wasn't that enough? Jack reached his locker, unlocked it and took some books out. As he put his skateboard in their place, he could hear the few lingering students *whispering* about someone.

"Luke Finnegan is so damn hot. I envy Trish."

"Yeah, but other girls are still able to get all over him."

"I heard a guy asked him out once."

"I mean, he is the vice principal's son, who wouldn't want to date him?" Jack rolled his eyes and walked to the second floor. All he'd been hearing about was Luke Finnegan. The most popular guy in Thomas Pry. The fencing king! Not to mention his family practically ran the school what with his father being vp. Jack walked into his class, quickly making his way to his seat next to the one and only.

"Alright, class," his teacher began. Jack knew her eyes were on him as she did roll call, but he pulled his books out and tried not to make too much noise as he searched for a pen. "Last week, we left off on Tutankhamen." His teacher's voice began to fade as Luke looked down at his phone, lying on his textbook. "Luke, could you put the phone away."

"I'm taking notes on here since I don't have my notebook. You can continue," he responded, his deep, raspy voice getting everyone's attention. Jack looked at the teacher and she rubbed her forehead.

"Every week, it's a new excuse with you," she replied. She put her hand on her hips and asked, "Which one will it be next week?"

"Just teach," Trish grumbled, rolling her eyes.

"Here." Everyone's head turned, and they watched as Jack placed a pen and paper on Luke's desk. Luke looked at him with confusion, but a smirk emerged on his face. Jack quickly looked to the front of the class.

"Thank you, Jack. Now, let's continue with the class." Luke was about to pick up the pen when Trish slid it to the side.

She placed a pen and notebook on his desk and whispered, "Use these. He's poor, he might need those." Jack scoffed but continued to listen to the lecture.

Luke pulled away from Trish and smiled at her. He licked his lower lip, still tasting her watermelon gloss. If he remembered correctly, Trish talked to him at a party last year and before he knew it, they were dating.

"You wanna meet in front of the school after your match?" Trish asked, snapping him out of reminiscing.

"Yeah, that works," he replied, pulling her closer.

"Uh…" Luke turned his head and stared at the brunet standing next to him. "You're blocking my locker," Jack said.

"Oh," Luke replied softly, Jack's smooth tone catching him off guard. Before he could move, Trish pulled him into another kiss.

"Guess you'll have to wait," she sighed, going in for a third. Jack stared at them before rolling his eyes and turning away. Guess he'll be carrying his books for the rest of the day. Luke pulled out of Trish's hold and watched Jack. "What?" Trish questioned, looking up at her boyfriend.

"His name's Jack, right?"

Lunchtime rolled around and once again, Jack isolated himself in the corner of a table far away from the loud students. He tried talking to some people the first week he got there, but they all looked at him like he was crazy. So rather than mope around, he buried his face in his book and tried to ignore the world around him.

"We stayed on the yacht for a day or two after the party," Luke explained. Students gathered at his lunch table for his usual stories.

"Was it really in Spain?" a guy asked.

"I've only been there once, but it's amazing," a girl commented.

"Yeah," Trish answered. "It was pretty amazing." She kissed her boyfriend and he smiled at her.

"So, what are you gonna do for your birthday next year?"

Luke sighed and pondered before replying, "I'll probably ask my parents to let me go to Japan."

"Oh, that's sick," Luke smiled at his friend. He and Gabriel had known each other since primary school. What started for them as an argument about who's half of a cookie was bigger turned into an everlasting friendship.

"Can you do something for me?" he suddenly asked, everyone else too distracted in their discussions about Japan.

Gabriel nodded. "What ya need?"

Jack rolled his eyes as the cafeteria noise made him lose his place.

"Hey!" He jumped; the voice way too close to his ear. Jack turned his head and the ginger-haired guy smiled. "What ya readin?" Jack just stared at him. Why the hell was he so close? "Oh, sorry. I'm Gabriel, but most people call me Gabe." He sat next to Jack and waited patiently for his response.

Jack contemplated on whether to answer or to ignore him, before saying, "Jack...and it's The Six Moons in Spring." Gabriel reached out his hand to look at the blurb, but Jack pulled the book away, holding it close to his face.

"Sorry." Gabriel looked around and his eyes caught Luke's. The other waved his hand as if telling him to go on. "Hey, are you going to the fencing match tonight?" Jack glanced up from his book before shaking his head.

"I have to start my English essay," he muttered.

"C'mon, it'll be fun!" Gabriel attempted to reassure. "Plus, it'll be your first one, right? I'll even sit with you." Jack huffed and nodded.

"Alright...I'll go." Something definitely felt odd about this encounter, but he didn't want to rule it out just yet.

Luke stood as the bell rang, announcing the end of the period. He spotted Jack zooming past everyone, and he could feel a smirk appearing on his face.

"What are you smiling about?" Trish questioned, looking at her boyfriend with confusion.

Luke snapped out of his daze and looked at Trish, suddenly kissing her roughly. "N-Nothing."

The fencing match was about to start. Jack walked in and looked around. Gabriel told him to meet here, but where was he? Jack huffed. He had ginger hair, right?

"Jack!" Jack groaned as all heads turned to him. He moved his legs quickly, making his way up the bleachers, and across the second row. "You made it."

Jack raised his brows and huffed, "Yep." He sat down, placing his bag between his legs, and watched as more students filed in through the gym doors.

"So, did they have fencing at…" Gabriel asked.

"Middleton?" Jack looked at the strip and nodded. "My uh…ex played."

"Oh, so you're like an expert," Gabriel cheerfully replied.

"I guess." The referee walked out and behind him were the competing school and Thomas Pry. The room filled with exaggerated cheers and Jack felt an unwanted but familiar chill up his spine. He watched as they saluted, and the first pair stood on the strip. As the matches proceeded, Jack could remember the adrenaline he felt when he'd watch.

"Fence!" Jack shook his head and wiped his face. He tried to remind himself in his head that he came here to get away from his ex. His eyes caught Luke who sat patiently on the sidelines, awaiting his turn.

Luke looked at the brunet and smiled. Jack gave him a small smile and averted his eyes.

"Luke's our best player," Gabriel exclaimed, grabbing Jack's attention. He only nodded, letting his eyes linger back to the fencing strip. It wasn't long before Luke was on the strip and Jack chuckled, covering his ears as the gym was filled with yelling and cheering again.

Luke lowered his mask and leaned back. The referee shouted at them to begin and in one swift motion, the tip of his foil was pressed against his opponent's uniform. There was a few claps before the fencers reset their positions. And Jack felt a surge of excitement try to sneak out again.

"And the winner of today's match is," the referee began. All six pairs had competed and now it was time for the results. "Thomas Pry High School!" The room filled with cheers again and Jack found himself out of his seat, clapping.

"See!" Gabriel exclaimed. Jack looked at him and Gabriel was cheesing. "I told you you'd have fun." Jack rolled his eyes, a smile emerging on his face.

"Party at my place!" Luke shouted. Jack gulped, clasping his hands after one last clap.

"Bye," he said, grabbing his bag.

"Woah, where are you going?" Gabriel asked, grabbing the string on the other's bag.

"Gotta study," Jack lied.

Gabriel stood and pointed out, "C'mon, Luke's parties are always fun. And, you can make some friends."

"I have friends." Gabriel scowled at Jack. Shit. Jack rolled his eyes and put his bag on his shoulder.

"Let me grab my skateboard."

"Yes!"

Luke ran his fingers through his hair, looking himself over in the mirror. He changed into tan shorts, a white top, and white vans. He made his way downstairs as he heard the sound of cars parking and people talking. Luke stood to the right of the front door, his maids and butlers on the left.

"Are you ready, Luke?" Patricia asked him.

Luke nodded and replied, "Open the door." Patricia nodded and another maid pulled the heavy oak doors open. "The party's out back!" As his classmates flooded in, he gave hugs, fist bumps, and hellos.

"We're here," Gabriel said, parking in front of the house. Jack looked out the window and gulped again. Gabriel turned off the car and got out. He walked around it and stared at Jack. "Well?" Jack bit the inside of his mouth and his eyes casted back on the large, white bricked house. He was here to make friends. To make friends. Jack stepped out of the car and closed the door behind him.

"Hey!" Luke greeted, watching Jack and Gabe walk in. Gabe pulled Luke into a hug, patting his back.

"Your jacket, sir?" a maid asked Jack. He stepped back, bumping into Gabe.

"N-no, thank you," he replied.

"Oh, Luke," Gabe began. He pulled Jack close and into a headlock. "You know Jack." Jack pulled out of the other's hold and scowled at him.

Luke smiled and responded, "You're in my history class, right?"

"Yeah." The three stared at each other before Jack turned his head.

"Well, welcome to Thomas Pry and welcome to my place." Luke rested his arm across Gabe's shoulders and smiled at Jack. "Let's head to the back." As they walked toward the loud music and rowdy teenagers, Luke pulled Gabe closer. "Thanks for convincing him."

Gabe smiled and asked, "Why are you so interested in him anyway?"

Luke shrugged and bluntly answered, "He's new and I wanna see what he's all about." Jack stared at the two as they walked ahead of him. When they reached the backyard, his eyes immediately caught the mini bar.

"Can I get a coke?" he asked the bartender. The woman nodded and poured the soda in a cup, and then splashed some sort of alcohol into it.

"Here you go," she said, handing it to him.

"Thanks." It wasn't exactly what he wanted, but he never turned down alcohol. He shifted in his seat at the bar. and watched people dancing and jumping into the swimming pool.

"You're the new kid, right?" a girl asked, startling Jack.

"Yeah…Jack Whyte," he responded.

"Are you in year 11?" another girl questioned.

"I'm in year 13, just like you. You guys have just been in your own world," he explained. He turned away and rested his hand under his chin, sipping on his drink. "Everyone has." The girls stared at him for a while before tapping his shoulder.

"So why the hell are you even here?"

Jack shrugged and said, "I figured I'd try to make friends. And Gabriel convinced me to come."

"You know Gabriel? Like Luke Finnegan's Gabriel?" Jack nodded and the girls scoffed.

"Are you girls teasing my friend?" Jack turned his head and smiled at him. The girls rolled their eyes and walked off.

"You know them?" Jack asked.

Gabriel nodded and confessed, "I may have slept with them and never called back."

"Wow." Jack shook his head and took another sip of his drink.

Luke looked at the bar and found himself smiling as Jack laughed.

"Why the fuck is Gabriel talking to that kid?" Luke glanced at Trish before shaking his head.

"I asked him to talk to him so he felt welcomed. Plus," Luke stood from his seat on the lounge chair and looked at Trish. "He seems like a cool guy." He made his way around the pool and over to the bar. "What you guys talking about?" he asked, watching Gabe and Jack laugh some more.

Jack looked up at him before quickly looking away. "U-Uh…nothing in particular."

"We were talking about you," Gabe blurted out. Luke smirked and put his hands on his hips.

"And what exactly were you telling Jack?"

"Just the usual embarrassing things."

"Ah."

"Everyone always talks about how great you are," Jack began, finally looking at Luke again. "So, it was nice to hear about the shitty parts of your personality."

"Wow." Luke looked at Gabe and the other slowly turned away. "Well, why don't I tell you some things about this asshole." Luke put Gabe in a chokehold and the other tapped his arm.

"Hey, new kid!" Jack turned his head and looked at the two guys approaching him. "Come swim with us," one suggested.

Jack shook his head and replied, "No, thanks." Luke let Gabe go and they began undressing. Jack watched them, but when his eyes caught Luke's, he quickly looked away. Damn. He really was hot.

"Come on," Gabriel said.

"You can't get me this time." Gabriel pouted before walking toward the pool.

"Alright, boys," Luke announced. Jack went to turn back to the bar, pulling out his phone, when he felt an arm around the front of his waist. He let the metal fall onto the bar and before he knew it, he was being rushed toward the pool.

"No! Put me down!" he yelled. "I can't—" But before Jack could finish his sentence, his body was surrounded by water. It was floating among the expert swimmers. Shit! His arms tried to get him to the surface, but his brain was already panicking.

Luke came up from under the water and was welcomed by cheers. He smiled and looked around. "Where is he?" He looked down and his heart's pace picked up. Luke delved back under, moving as quickly as he could.

Jack could feel arms wrap around his waist and his body moved through the water. Luke pulled Jack up and Gabe helped him, pulling him out of the pool. Jack began coughing up liquid and he opened his eyes.

"Are you okay?" He stared at Luke before shoving him back into the water.

"You fucking asshole. I can't fucking swim," he yelled. He stood, took off his jacket and shirt and stormed off. Luke came back up and looked at Gabe. The other watched him before jogging into the house.

"Jack!" Jack halted halfway through the hall and huffed. Goddammit. Gabriel stood in front of him, holding his hips as he tried to catch his breath. "I'll…drive you home." Jack closed his eyes and huffed.

"Thanks." He walked past Gabe and the other followed behind him.

"Jack," Luke panted, but Jack and Gabe were already walking out the front door. He groaned, running his hands down his face.

"Hey," Luke moved his hands and looked at the girl in front of him. "Come back to the party." He looked at the front door and huffed. He rested his arm across Trish's shoulders, and they turned to the backyard.

"Thanks," Jack muttered. He went to reach for his things in the backseat when Gabriel held his arm.

"He's not terrible you know," he said. He moved his hand back to the wheel and huffed. "He probably feels like a total ass right now."

"Sure." Jack grabbed his things and got out of the car.

"See you t-okay," Gabriel said, Jack slamming the door in his face. He walked up the steps of his two-story home and unlocked the door. He made his way to his room, tossing his bag and skateboard on the floor. Fucking asshole. He pulled off his clothes and changed into shorts and a t-shirt. Asshole. Jack grabbed all of his wet clothes and made his way to the laundry room.

"Jack?" He slowly turned and saw his mother standing in the doorway. "How was the..." She saw the wet clothes in his hands and looked at him with confusion. "What happened?"

Jack forced himself to chuckle and answered, "I was tossed in the water and almost died." He tried to laugh it off, but the fear from the memory brought tears to his eyes.

"Sweetie," his mother moped, pulling him into a hug. "Who did it? I'll call their parents right now."

Jack waved her off and reassured, "It's fine, Mom. It was my fault for going to the stupid party in the first place." His mother let off a long sigh before kissing his forehead.

"Don't talk to those kids again, Jack."

"But I won't have any friends, mom. I'm not gonna just go to class, come home, and study. I want to make friends."

"I understand that Jack, but don't forget that your priority is your education. If those kids aren't treating you right, forget about them." Jack put his clothes in the washing machine and turned it on.

"I'm going to bed," he mumbled. His mother reached out to him, and he pulled away.

He knew he got distracted last year. But his friends...Jack huffed and ran his fingers through his hair, plopping down on his bed. It wasn't his fault his ex was a manipulative piece of shit.

"Ugh!"

Luke sighed and looked at Trish who lied down beside him. The party ended two hours ago. He'd been trying to go to sleep, but he couldn't stop thinking about Jack. He felt like such an asshole! He should've paid attention to him. What if he died at the party? Luke wouldn't be able to live with himself. Luke took a deep breath, trying to calm himself down. He had to apologize. He had to.

Part 2

As Jack walked into school, all eyes were on him. Well, fuck. He could hear them whispering about the party.

"That kid almost drowned yesterday."

"I can't believe Luke almost killed him."

"Why'd he even come to the party?" Jack shook his head and walked over to his locker. He opened it and stuck his head in.

Luke chuckled at the action and slicked his hair back. He walked over to Jack and tapped his shoulder, smiling. "Hey," he greeted.

Jack jumped and hit his head on the locker. "Shit." He turned around and rolled his eyes. "What do you want?"

Luke huffed and apologized, "Look, I'm sorry alright. I didn't know you couldn't swim, and I should've never tossed you in the water." Jack felt his cheeks turning red and he looked away. What the hell is wrong with him? "How about we talk over some pizza, my treat." Pizza? Really?

Jack scoffed and replied, "Sure, why not." He turned back to his locker and grabbed his books.

"Cool, meet you by the fountain at three?" Luke exclaimed. Jack nodded and closed his locker before walking away. "Hey, let's go to class…" Luke watched the other walk off and couldn't help but smirk. Jack smiled as he heard the other sigh behind him and walked into the classroom behind the stairs. He took his seat and pulled a pen from his bag.

"Hey." He looked up and managed a smile.

"Hey, Gabriel," he greeted back. Gabriel sat beside him.

"Are you feeling okay?" he asked, resting a hand on the other's shoulder.

Jack shrugged, looking over his notes, and answered, "I've been better." Gabriel stared at the brunet before nodding.

"Okay." He looked over at the door and smiled.

"Hey, guys," Luke greeted. He and Gabe shared a handshake before he sat on the other side of Jack. He glanced at him, but Jack was still looking at his notebook. He's not half-bad looking. Luke smirked as Jack smiled. That dimple's cute too. Luke gulped as Jack glanced at him before looking straight ahead. He only liked girls…right? Luke pressed his fingers against his temples and huffed. Did he lose his mind? He shook his head and reached into his bag for a pen. "Hey, Jack," he called out. He couldn't find one in the crevasses of the pockets. Jack turned to him and waited for him to continue. "Can you let me borrow a pen?"

"Yeah," Jack dug into his bag and handed the pen to Luke. He looked at him and they smiled at each other, their fingers brushing.

"Thanks." Gabe smirked at them, looking back at his book.

Luke looked at his phone and huffed. He was standing next to the fountain, still waiting for Jack. Where the hell was he?

Jack jogged down the school stairs and to the fountain, tapping Luke on the shoulder. "Hey."

"Well, it's about fucking time you got here. It's already three thirty," Jack rolled his eyes.

"I had to ask my teacher a couple questions," Jack replied. Luke looked at him from the corner of his eye before huffing and patting Jack's head.

"Such a good student," he teased. "Let's go get pizza." Jack nodded, ignoring the comment, and followed Luke. "This place is pretty good." It was silent as they walked to the pizzeria. Luke glanced at Jack before asking, "Why'd you-uh…Why'd you transfer?"

Jack shrugged. "You want the truth…or the lie?" Luke looked at him and furrowed his brows.

"The lie?" Was it really so bad that he had to come up with one?

Jack huffed, "My parents found better job offers so we had to move."

"Okay…Now the truth." Damn, he should've just told him the lie and be done with it. They arrived at the pizzeria and Luke turned to Jack. "What do you want?"

"A Sicilian is fine."

Luke couldn't help but smile and responded, "Great minds think alike." Jack went to say something, but Luke was already ordering their pizza. "So," he suddenly said, his eyes back on Jack. "The truth."

Jack nodded, leaning against the tiled pillar beside him, and explained, "My ex was pretty rich, and his parents were able to get me kicked out of the school. But, thankfully, they gave me the option to transfer so I took it."

"Wait, so you got kicked out two weeks ago?"

"No, I was kicked out at year 11, but they let me finish my 12th year there before I transferred. And then Thomas Pry allowed me to come a few weeks after school started."

"Damn, what a fucked-up ex."

"Tell me about it." His friends stopped talking to him because of that asshole. Jack huffed and crossed his arms. He and Luke stood there in silence again, patiently waiting while their food was being warmed.

"Two Sicilians," the cashier called out. Luke walked up to him and grabbed the pizzas.

He turned back to Jack and smiled. "Let's find a seat." Jack nodded and looked around at the green booths. He picked one by a window and sat down. Luke slid into the booth, sitting across from him. He passed the other a slice and said, "Here you go." Jack took the pizza and took a bite of the slice, the thick dough deflating in his mouth.

"Thanks," he muffled, pulling the pizza away as the mozzarella stretched. Luke watched him and a small smile could be seen past the slice in his mouth. Jack caught him and furrowed his brows. "What?"

The other took a bite of his slice, quickly averting his eyes before saying, "I uh…I really felt like shit for tossing you in the water."

"Oh, so you don't feel bad anymore?" Jack teased.

Luke waved his hands and protested, "N-No, I still do." He huffed. "I know I already said it, but I'm really fucking sorry." Jack smiled and he sighed.

"I accept your apology." He looked out the window and took another bite of his pizza. "I really thought you were gonna be a real prick from the way people talked about you." Now he looked at Luke. "But you're kinda cool."

Luke licked his lips as his muscles moved into a smile and replied, "You're not too bad yourself." Jack rolled his eyes, a smile still on his face, and he continued eating his pizza. "You really like pizza huh?"

Jack nodded, gulped, and pointed out, "It's been a while since I had a good slice."

"Well…maybe this can be our regular thing."

"Oh, so we're friends now." Luke shrugged.

"I mean, not yet, but we can become friends. We can come here every once and a while for lunch, learn about each other's deepest, darkest secrets." What the hell was it about this guy that even made him suggest that? Jack shrugged back, wiping his mouth.

"Sounds like a plan."

"Oh, and don't worry, I'll cover us." Jack couldn't let those words fly and he smirked.

"So, I'm your date now?" Luke coughed as the cheese began going down the wrong tube. He pulled it from his mouth and coughed some more. "Shit, you okay? I was just joking." Luke nodded and grabbed his water bottle, gulping down the liquid.

"I-I'm fine," he breathed. He had his fair share of guys come onto him, but he never felt his heart move like that. "Phew."

"It was cool talking to you," Jack confessed, looking up at Luke. They stood outside the pizzeria, ready to part ways.

"Same here," Luke responded. "Do you uh, need a ride?" Jack shook his head and held up his skateboard.

"I've got this bad boy." Luke chuckled and shrugged.

"Alright, suit yourself." He pulled out his phone. "Here, put your number in."

"For?"

"So we can keep in touch." Jack stared at Luke. Did he seriously land a friend from almost dying? He hesitated a little longer before taking the phone and entering his number.

"Here you go." Luke looked at the contact and furrowed his brows.

"Where's your picture?"

"I don't wanna take one." Luke quickly raised his phone and took a picture of Jack. "Dude, what the fuck?"

"What? I need to make sure I'm texting the right Jack."

"Gimme your phone." Jack reached out and grabbed it. He deleted the photo and huffed, taking a picture of himself. "There. Now you'll know," he chuckled. Luke took his phone back and saved the contact.

"Alright, well," He looked back at Jack. "See you at school tomorrow?"

"Yep." Jack put down his skateboard and got on. He looked back at Luke. "Later." As he began skating off, a car drove past him.

"Ralph?" Luke exclaimed, furrowing his brows. He walked up to the car and stared at the middle-aged man with ginger-salted hair. "I didn't even call you yet."

"She insisted we come get you," Ralph explained. He leaned closer to Luke. "And you know how much I can't stand taking orders from people outside the family." Now he glanced at the back of the limo and shook his head.

"I heard that," the girl said.

"Good for you."

"Trish?" Luke really didn't feel like being bothered by her nonsense. She emerged from the back and smiled.

"Hey babe!"

Luke smiled and joked, "Next time, no matter what she says, don't let her in. Just drive away." Trish tried to reach over and hit Luke, but he backed up. He made his way to the back seat and got in.

Trish hit him and said, "You've been a total dick today."

Luke scoffed, "How?"

"You haven't talked to me all day, and when I finally do see you, you act like an asshole." This was the one thing he couldn't stand about Trish. She always acted like she was the center of the universe.

"We don't have class together, and I told you I was hanging out with Jack today."

"Who? That poor guy?"

"He's not poor."

"Well, his parents aren't rich."

"And neither were yours, until a couple months ago." Luke shook his head and looked out the window. "Shit."

"You're a fucking asshole!"

"Thanks. Ralph, stop the car."

"With pleasure."

"What the hell are you doing?" Trish asked as Luke took her bag and handed it to her.

"Get out," he ordered. She stared at him before slapping him.

"Dick," she growled. She got out of the car, slamming the door.

"Ralph, take me home."

Ralph looked at him before saying, "Of course."

Jack hummed as he made himself a tuna sandwich for dinner. It wasn't much, but it was better than letting his stomach argue with him all night. His father walked into the kitchen and shagged his hair.

"And what are you so happy about?" he asked, leaning against the counter.

Jack turned to his father and replied, "I think I made a friend…or two."

"That's great, kiddo." His father made his way over to the fridge and grabbed a small container of food. He looked at Jack and smiled at him. "I'm off to work." Jack nodded and waved at his dad before heading upstairs to his room with his sandwich. He pulled his book from his bag and began reading.

Luke watched as his mother and father walked into the dining room and sat down at the table. The butler began bringing in their food, Patricia serving wine and water.

"So, son, how was your day?" Luke's father asked.

Luke shrugged and answered, "I apologized to the new kid today. He's actually a really cool guy."

His mother questioned, "What's his name?"

"Jack Whyte," his father responded before he could. "I don't want you talking to that boy."

"Why not?" Did this have something to do with that other school? Luke knew it was serious, but was it so bad that even his father didn't want them talking?

"He caused a lot of trouble for the Williams family at his old school. And I will not have a repeat."

"Is that the truth or what they told you?" Luke blurted out.

His father slammed his hand on the table and ordered, "You are not to question my words." Luke huffed and looked down at his plate.

"I'm sorry."

"What else did you do today?" his mother asked, breaking the silence before it could appear.

Luke shrugged and replied, "I fought with Trish."

"What about?"

"You and that girl are always arguing," his father mumbled, shoving salmon into his mouth.

Luke huffed, "She was just being a hypocrite."

"Well, make up with her soon, okay?" Luke nodded and he smiled at his mom.

11:00 pm

Jack groaned as he heard his message ringtone. He clawed at his desk and grabbed his phone.

Hey!

"Who the fuck is this?" He rolled his eyes and put the phone back. Two more buzzes.

Ure not gonna respond?

Jack sat up and began texting, his thumbs slamming against the screen.

> **Who the fuck is this and how the fuck did you get me # and y the fuck r u texting me so late!!!**

It's Luke…

Jack fell back on his bed and groaned. He completely forgot he gave Luke his number. But why the hell was he texting so late?

> **Sorry, I completely forgot**

Jack couldn't help but smirk at the photo. It was Luke, giving a thumbs up with no shirt on.

> **U sure ur gf won't get mad about this pic?**

Don't worry, she has it

Luke stared at the screen, watching the three dancing dots.

So what ya doin?

> **I was tryin to sleep until u woke me up!**

Sorry bout that…
how about I pick u up tmm morning

Um…
No thx
Itll be weird

How?

IDK
Maybe bc we barely know each other…

Come oooooooonnnnnn

Nah

Okay, think of it as an apology for waking u

Alright! Alright

See u tmm morning then!
Oh and send me your address.
Maybe we can hang out after school?

Goodnight

Luke smiled and placed his phone on his dresser. He closed his curtains and walked over to his bed. They'd be friends before he knew it.

Jack groaned and rolled over in bed. *In my American Apparel*-He quickly hit snooze and rolled back over. Two more minutes, then he'd get up. His eyes were heavy again, and he could feel himself drifting.

"Jack, sweetie." Jack's eyes shot open, and he groaned again. "You have to get up."

"Two more minutes." He put his cover over his head, but he could hear his mom getting closer.

"There's a kid outside saying he came to pick you up." Jack slowly opened his eyes and began fighting his covers. He forgot he agreed to be chauffeured today.

"Ugh," he whined. He reached for his phone and his mom did him a favor, putting it in his hand. "Thanks."

Morning! I'm downstairs

I know
Gimme 10min

Alright

Luke looked up at Ralph and said, "He needs ten minutes."

Ralph looked back at him and asked, "What is he going to do in ten minutes? Brush the top row of his teeth?" He shook his head and tapped his finger on the wheel to the beat coming from the radio.

Jack tossed his toothbrush back in its cup on the sink and checked his jacket for any toothpaste. Thankfully, he convinced himself to take a shower last night, so it was one less thing for him to do. He walked into his room and grabbed his skateboard and bag.

"You're ready?" his mom asked. Jack nodded and walked over to her by his bedroom doorway.

"Later, Mom," he said kissing her cheek and rubbing her belly. She smiled at him and watched him rush down the stairs and out the door.

"That was fifteen minutes, lad," Ralph called out.

Luke moved over in the car and reassured, "Don't worry about it, Jack, Ralph is just a grumpy old man in the morning."

"Same here." Jack chuckled. Ralph smiled at him and started driving.

"Your tie is messed up," Luke pointed out, reaching for Jack's tie. Jack watched Luke as he fixed it for him.

"Thanks," he muttered. Luke looked up and their eyes met.

"Uh." He moved back and looked out the window. "Did you eat breakfast?"

"How the hell would I have time for breakfast?" Jack questioned.

"Well, shit, I was just making conversation."

The other huffed and nodded. "I'm sorry, I didn't mean to snap at you."

"It's alright," Luke started. "You're a grumpy old man, remember?" Jack chuckled and shook his head.

When they finally got to school, Jack got out first, Luke following behind him. Well shit.

Luke looked at Jack with confusion and asked, "What's wrong?"

Jack huffed. "Everyone's staring holes into me." He began walking toward the school stairs and Luke was close behind.

"Does it bother you that much?" Jack shook his head and jogged up the steps.

"It's just annoying as hell."

"Hey!" Gabe suddenly exclaimed, startling them. "What are you two doing walking together?" He rested his arms across both their shoulders, all three teens walking into Thomas Pry.

"I offered him a ride last night," Luke answered.

"After he woke me up," Jack clarified, pulling out of Gabriel's hold.

"First of all, that sounded like you two spent the night together. Second, you've never offered me a ride," Gabe complained.

"You have a car," Luke replied, ignoring the first half of the comment. He walked over to his locker that was two away from Jack's and grabbed his books.

"So what?" Jack closed his locker and was headed for the stairs when Luke grabbed his arm.

"Wait for me?" He rolled his eyes and stood beside Gabe while they spoke. "Jack and I are hanging out later, wanna join?" Luke asked, closing his locker.

Gabe huffed. "I can't. I have swim meet today. But I'm down for the next time you hang out." They all began walking to and up the stairs. "I'll see you guys."

"Yep," Jack muttered. He and Luke walked into their classroom and took their regular seats. Luke sighed before looking at Trish. She had her arms crossed and she was staring straight ahead.

"Let me guess, you're sorry because you were a complete asshole and now you want me back," Trish concluded. Luke stared at her before laughing.

"You know what, I was gonna apologize, but I change my mind," he replied, and turned to Jack.

"Luke," she called out.

"What do you wanna do later?" he asked Jack, getting the other's attention.

"I don't know," he replied, putting his books down and looking at Luke. "You play video games?"

"Luke!" Jack glanced over Luke's shoulder, but the other moved so he couldn't see Trish anymore.

"Yeah, we can play whatever you want."

"Luke, you fucking prick!" Trish yelled, standing.

"Ms. Griffith, please have a seat," the teacher ordered. "We are beginning our class." Luke watched from the corner of his eye as Trish sat down, but he didn't turn to look at her.

Luke stared at Jack from across the room, drowning out the loud talking around him.

"Go get him," he ordered, glancing at Gabe who sat beside him at the lunch table.

Gabe looked at him and asked, "Why do I have to go get him, I'm not your-oh, is that a hundred bucks?" Luke smirked and the other shoved him. "You do it," he said bluntly. Luke pouted and Gabe rolled his eyes. "I'll be right back." He got up and made his way over to Jack.

Jack looked up from his book and smiled. "Hey." Gabe sat beside him and huffed.

"Luke wants you to come sit with us."

Jack chuckled. "I'm good. They're not gonna be welcoming."

"Who gives a fuck if they aren't?" Gabe began. "You're our friend, everyone has no choice but to like you. You're pretty awesome might I add." Jack scoffed, unable to hide his smile. Why not make him wait a little.

"Mm, I don't know." Gabe gawked and groaned.

Luke looked at Gabe and the other shook his head.

"Luke?" a girl sitting beside him said. Luke looked at her and stood.

"I'll be back," he replied. He made his way over to Gabe and Jack, sitting across from them. "Why are you sitting by yourself, dude?" he asked.

Jack looked at him and huffed. "Because I like to sit where I'm not being constantly judged."

"Oh please, just ignore them," Luke responded.

"That's what I said," Gabe exclaimed. Jack shook his head and looked back at his book.

"What are you reading?" Luke questioned, taking it from his hands.

"What the hell?" Jack went to grab it back, but Luke turned away.

"What the hell is this?" he muttered. "His hand moved up his leg, past the ropes that bound his body, and he grabbed his swinging..." He went silent, but his eyes continued to read. Sure, he'd seen guys kiss, but this was more intense. He handed the book back to Jack and ran his hands up his face, covering it.

"Did you like what you read?" Jack teased, seeing the other's cheeks turning red.

"I…I don't know." Now his fingers ran through his hair, and he huffed. Jack was about to say something when Luke raised his hand. "Don't…say anything else. I shouldn't have taken the book."

Gabe grabbed the book now, asking, "What did you…oh…oh!" He quickly handed it to Jack. "How can you be into this stuff?"

"It's well written," Jack pointed out.

"But you're…into that stuff? Like…tying people up?" Luke questioned.

Jack smirked and answered, "And if I am? Why not try something new?"

"N-No, you're totally right. I just never expected to learn something like that about you." Jack shrugged and continued reading.

"Ya learn something new every day."

After school, Jack and Luke headed to the Finnegan residence. The car stopped in front of the house and Luke got out first, Jack coming out right after.

"I'll see you lads tomorrow," Ralph called out. Luke waved at him before walking to the front door.

Patricia opened it and greeted, "Hello, Luke, and…"

Luke pointed at Jack and introduced him "This is Jack Whyte."

"Nice to meet you, Jack," Patricia said with a smile. Jack smiled back and followed Luke to the living room. He stood in the doorway and took in the décor. The walls were painted plain white, covered with large, gold-framed art.

"That TV is ridiculous," Jack commented. The enormous television that claimed one wall sat between two columns that had etchings of what looked like angels.

Luke nodded and responded, "I know." He grabbed Jack's hand and pulled him along, sitting down. Jack stared at him, then at his hand. "Oh," Luke pulled his hand away and got up. "What uh, what do you wanna play?"

Jack sat back in his seat and replied, "Do you have anything with multiplayer, online missions?"

"Yep." He went ahead and turned on the television, putting in the game. He passed Jack a controller and plopped down beside him. As they played, Luke tried to think of things to talk about.

"Do you have any siblings?" he asked.

Jack nodded and answered, "My mom is pregnant with a girl, so I'll have a little sister in a couple months. What about you?"

"Only child." Luke vigorously pressed the button on his controller, sitting up in his seat. "When's your birthday?"

"The eighth of October." Jack muttered and he inched closer to the edge of the couch, his fingers still tapping the a-button."

"Isn't that in a week?"

"Four days actually."

"Are you doing anything?"

"No…why?" Luke paused the game and looked at Jack.

"Why don't you throw a birthday party at my place. I'll cover everything."

Jack rolled his eyes and shook his head. "And why would you wanna do that?"

"Because you're my friend and it's gonna be worth spending the money on you." Jack couldn't help it, and he began laughing. "What's so funny?"

"I feel like an escort." He laughed. He slouched in the chair and huffed, putting the game back on. "Thanks for the offer, but no."

"Well, what if it's a small party?"

"No."

"If it's just you, Gabe, and I?"

"No." Luke paused the game again.

"Okay, what if I just buy you something?"

"Argh! Alright!" Jack yelled. "Do whatever you want." Luke smirked and turned the game back on. "You're so fucking annoying," Jack grumbled.

"I know."

Jack stepped out of the car, grabbing his bag and skateboard.

"Thanks," he told the driver. Luke tried to convince him to let Ralph drive him home, but he refused, taking a taxi instead. He walked to the front door, unlocked it, and headed upstairs.

"You're home, sweetie?" he heard his mom call.

"Yeah, I'm gonna take a shower," Jack replied.

"Did you eat dinner?"

"Yeah." He dropped his bag and skateboard on his bedroom floor and began undressing. He felt his pants buzz and pulled out his phone.

Did you get home safely?

Yes, y?

U worried?

Shouldn't I be?

Maybe

Should he send a winky face? Jack stared at the text before scoffing. Who was he kidding?

What you doin tmm?

Sleeping in
It's the wknd

Exactly
We can go shopping

For what

U
Ur bday

No!

But u said I could do whatever I wanted

"Goddammit." Jack huffed and began texting. Why was he so agreeable?

What time?

Like noon?

Sure 😑

Alright, c u then 😎

Luke put his phone away and lied back on his bed.

Jack looked around and pouted. He sat near a café in the mall, waiting patiently for Luke. He pulled on his black sweater and huffed.

"Were you waiting long?" Jack looked up and smirked. Luke smiled at him, taking off his sunglasses.

The other stood and answered, "No."

"Okay, good. Ready?" Luke exclaimed, putting his sunglasses in his jean's pocket. Jack nodded and stood, walking beside him. "What are you gonna buy?"

"I don't know, a t-shirt?" Jack replied. "Plus, didn't you say you were gonna buy it for me?"

"Oh, so you remembered that?"

Jack shrugged and said, "I remember what I want." Luke chuckled and walked into the large clothing store beside them, Jack close behind. It barely had any clothing racks in it and when Jack looked at a price tag, all he could do was scoff. Luke watched Jack make his way to the 'sale' section before following behind him. Jack sifted through the overpriced sweaters and shirts, glancing at Luke as he stood beside him. "You getting anything?" he asked, pulling out a black sweater covered in splashed roses.

"Just a jacket and some pants. I gotta look good for your birthday too." Jack chuckled, pulling the sweater from the rack.

"You look good no matter what you wear," he muttered. Luke's head shot up from the clothes in front of him and Jack couldn't help but smile. He walked off and Luke just stared at him.

"Did you just say I look hot all the time?" He usually didn't entertain flirtation from guys, but there was just something about Jack. He followed quickly behind him and asked, "You want anything else?"

Jack shook his head and responded, "Nah, I'm not much of a shopper anyway."

"Alright." Luke continued to look for some clothes and when he finally talked Jack's ear off, they made their way to the registers.

"Next," the cashier called out. Luke stepped forward, but Jack wasn't following him.

"Jack," Luke said.

"What?"

"Come here," he ordered.

"No. I got it." Luke walked over to Jack and grabbed the sweater from him.

"Hi, how are you?" the cashier greeted, beginning to scan their clothes.

"I'm gonna buy it," Jack muttered.

"I'm good, and how are you?" Luke answered, ignoring him. The cashier put everything in a bag and looked at the computer. "Your total is four hundred and forty-one dollars."

Jack pulled the hundred-dollar note from his pocket and shoved it in Luke's back pocket, saying, "Here." Luke shook his head and pulled out his wallet. He took out a black card, his name and card number covered in gold foil. Jack just stared in awe. This guy was loaded. Super fucking loaded.

"You can put the sweater and watch in another bag," Luke told the cashier.

"Sure."

"Wait, watch?" Jack asked, moving to Luke's side.

"Oh yeah, I got that for you."

"Luke," Jack huffed.

"What? It's a gift from me to you," Luke reassured. The cashier handed Luke his receipt and the bags and smiled at him.

"Have a great day." Luke smiled back and began walking out the store. Jack pulled on the other's arm, slowing him down.

"Oh, here." Jack took the bag, but his hand was still on Luke's arm. "What?" He pulled him to the side.

"Can I...can I ask you something?"

"You just did," Luke joked. Jack pouted and hit him. The other smirked, and they continued walking through the mall. "Ask away."

Jack huffed before asking, "Why are you being so nice to me? Is it because you just feel shitty about that party accident or do you wanna flaunt your wealth? Or do you actually care about me and want to be my friend?"

Luke stopped and turned to Jack. He stared at him with a smile before explaining, "When I first talked to you, I knew you were a cool guy. Yes, I felt like an ass because of the party and yes, I'm kinda using shopping as another way to make up for it. But I really do wanna be your friend and it's your birthday. It's the one day you should take advantage of people trying to spoil you." He smiled at Jack again and unintentionally bit his bottom lip. "Does that answer your question?"

Jack huffed and looked away, muttering, "Don't expect too much for your birthday." Luke chuckled and put his arm across Jack's shoulders.

"Let's go get lunch." Jack nodded and the two made their way to the food court.

Part 3

Jack looked at the flowers in the center of the art room before looking back at the canvas in front of him. His birthday was in a day, and he still had no clue what Luke had planned.

"So," Jack glanced at the girl on his left and sighed.

"Trish?" he muttered, his eyes back on his canvas.

"I hear Luke is throwing a birthday party for you." Well at least now he knew what was in store for tomorrow.

"I guess so." Trish rolled her eyes and sighed. She turned to Jack and forced her lips into a smile.

"Well, he asked me to find out what kind of cake you like. If you have any allergies," she continued.

"I haven't seen you guys talk since you yelled at him in history," Jack pointed out. Trish scoffed and shook her head.

"We fight like that all the time. We're good now." Jack stared at her before returning to his painting. "So what do you like?"

He put his brush down and said, "You two never give up huh?"

"Nope."

He huffed. "Chocolate anything. No peanuts because I'm allergic."

Trish smiled and nodded. "I'll let him know."

Luke swam from one end of the pool to the next. He'd been bragging all day about the party he planned for Jack.

"Are your parents really gonna let you throw it for him," Gabe asked, swimming beside Luke. "Wasn't your dad mad that you guys were becoming friends?"

Luke pushed his hair out of his face and replied, "They're in Paris for their anniversary so they don't really have a say." Gabe nodded and sighed.

"I can't believe Jack actually agreed to a party. We barely know him." Luke chuckled and scratched his head.

"Well, I haven't actually told him yet," he confessed. "I wanted it to be a surprise."

"And you thought telling everyone at school about the 'kickass party' you're gonna throw was a good idea?"

"Okay, so maybe it wasn't the best idea, but at least Jack can get to know more people."

"Wow," Gabe exclaimed. "I've never seen you give a shit about someone else this much." Now he stared at his friend and furrowed his brows. "Does Trish even know this side of you exists?"

Luke splashed the other and mumbled, "Asshole." Gabe laughed, splashing Luke back. But when his eyes looked up, he stopped.

"Speak of the devil." Luke turned his head, and his smile dropped.

"Can I talk to you?"

"Well, hello to you too," Luke said back and he went to turn away from her.

"Please." Please? That word only existed to Trish when she wanted money or more during sex.

Luke huffed and looked at her. "Meet me after class." She smiled and walked off, nearly slipping in her heels.

"You guys still haven't made up?" Gabe muttered. Luke shook his head and shrugged.

"It happens all the time." Gabe nodded and watched Luke swim across the pool before following him. He pushed his hair out of his face, furrowing his brows.

"Wasn't it about Jack?"

"No. She was just mad that I didn't hang out with her or something." Gabe mouthed an 'oh' and Luke pulled himself out of the water.

"Thanks, I'll see you later," Jack said. His day had been going pretty well. His classmates were talking to him and wishing him an early happy birthday, which he figured was Luke's doing. He was finally caught up in all his classes, and his teachers were praising him for his hard work. Jack turned the corner, heading toward the cafeteria.

"He said he liked chocolate and peanut butter anything," Trish informed.

Luke rolled his eyes and replied, "Is that all you wanted to tell me?" He went to walk past her, and he mumbled, "It was supposed to be a surprise."

Trish grabbed his arm and asked, "Why are you so obsessed with this guy? What about me? I'm your fucking girlfriend."

Luke huffed and turned back to her, explaining once again, "Because he's nice, honest, and he doesn't care about people's social status. He just wants friends, people he can trust and laugh with."

"Well, I'm trying to do better," Trish said. "That's why I asked him about his favorite kind of cake. I'm trying to get to know him." She grabbed her boyfriend's hands and pulled him close. "I'm trying to fix us." Luke stared at her and sighed.

Jack watched as the couple's lips met and he huffed. Well, there went his good day. He quickly stomped past them, barely hearing Luke as he called his name. When he entered the cafeteria, he found his seat by the window. He tossed his bag into the corner and pulled out The Six Moons in Spring. What did he expect? Luke was straight. Jack grumbled in his book, skimming the pages, and flipping them to the point where they almost fell out.

"Dude, you didn't see me wave at you when you walked in?" Jack looked up, and his anger only seemed to take up half of his mind's thoughts now. Gabe stood in front of him with his hands on his hips.

"Sorry, I was kind of in my own world," he replied.

The other took a seat and muffled, "I could see that." He watched Jack for a while before asking, "Are you excited about your party tomorrow?"

Jack managed a smirk and responded, "I told Luke he could do whatever he wanted, so I shouldn't have expected less." He looked out the window and huffed. "Kind of hoping he doesn't invite Trish."

"Not a fan of her?"

"No. She just needs him on her shoulder to feel important. She doesn't care about him." Gabe's eyes went wide, and Jack caught his reaction. "Wh-What?"

Gabe looked around and trailed off, "Do you…" Jack stared at him before his eyes went wide.

"Wh-What…What gave you that impression?" Had he been that easy to read?

"I mean, you're either talking about schoolwork or Luke. And you kind of just went on a jealous rant about his girlfriend." Jack groaned and covered his face with his book. "Aw, dude, look, it's totally fine. I think it's kinda cute, not saying I'm into that kind of thing but yeah." Jack glared at Gabe and the other chuckled. "Hey." He leaned in close and smirked. "Fuck Trish, she's been causing Luke trouble ever since they started dating. Plus, if you ask me, I think you two would make a pretty cool couple." Jack bit the inside of his mouth and huffed.

Luke spotted Gabe and Jack and he marched his way over, Trish following close behind.

"Hey," he greeted. Jack looked at him from his book before looking back down. "Why'd you ignore me earlier?" Jack didn't respond. Instead, he glanced at Gabe whose eyes began to roam. "Hello," Luke sang. He sat beside Gabe, Trish sitting beside him, and Jack told himself not to show his annoyance.

"What do you want?" he said a bit harshly.

"Wow, are you mad because I'm throwing you a birthday party?" Jack realized he was being a bit obnoxious. There was no reason to be mean to Luke, he didn't do anything wrong.

"No," he huffed. "I'm actually really happy." Jack finally looked at Luke and smiled. "It's been great getting everyone to wish me happy birthday."

Luke furrowed his brows and questioned, "So then why'd you ignore me?" Their eye contact was unbearable, and Jack looked back at his book.

"I guess I felt like teasing you a bit." He shrugged and glanced at Luke, receiving a smile.

"Well, I'll have you know, Trish here was telling me what kind of cake to get you." Trish shot a look at him, and she gulped. Gabe noticed this and he raised a brow.

"What is it, Trish?" he asked. She shifted in her seat, chuckling.

"Y-You'll find out tomorrow," she stuttered, now looking for her phone.

Luke shrugged and answered, "I mean, it's just chocolate and peanut butter. Pretty great combination." Jack slowly lowered his book and stared at Luke.

"What are you talking about?" he questioned. Maybe he heard wrong. There was no way Trish told him that.

Luke chuckled. "Isn't your favorite chocolate and peanut butter?" He glanced at Trish, and she was staring at her phone. She grabbed her bag and went to stand when Luke huffed, "You're kidding."

"I'm allergic to peanuts, so why the hell would peanut butter be my favorite anything?" Jack pointed out.

"What the actual fuck, Trish?" Luke yelled. "Were you trying to kill him?"

"It would've just been a sm-small reaction," she said, standing and waving her hands.

"Do you not know how serious a nut allergy is?" Gabe asked.

"What the hell is wrong with you?" Jack added.

"It's always about you!" Trish suddenly shouted. "It's only been two weeks and all he ever seems to care about is you." She scoffed. "What the hell is so great about some middle-classed prick who was kicked out of his last school?" she blurted out.

Jack shot Luke a look and he quickly raised his hands. "I never told her anything."

"Don't worry," Trish reassured. "I did my own research. My boyfriend was too busy sucking your dick to give two shits about what I was doing."

"You know what, you're right. I didn't give two shits. Because I'm not your fucking boyfriend."

"What?" At this point, most of the cafeteria was a part of their argument.

"I'm done with you. I've never met such a jealous, conniving, empty hearted person like you. We're done." Trish gritted her teeth, and she slapped him. She stormed off and Luke looked at everyone around them. "Sorry guys," he shouted. "But there'll be no party tomorrow." The students groaned and booed, returning to their seats.

"Hey," Jack said softly. Luke looked at him and huffed, rubbing his forehead.

"I'm sorry. I didn't know she would pull something like that," he apologized. She didn't even try to deny it. Jesus. Jack reached out his hand and rested it on Luke's. They looked at each other, staring for a while before smiling. Gabe who'd been watching everything unfold gently placed his hand on theirs. "Why don't we just hang out tomorrow.

Just the three of us," Luke suggested. He glanced at Jack, winked, and the other pulled his hand away.

"Um…yeah, that works," he muttered, picking his book back up.

Luke suggested, "I'll buy some alcohol and snacks. Guys night in?"

Gabe nodded and shouted, "Guys night in! Guys night in!" Jack chuckled behind his book, but his eyes were focused on Luke. The other smiled at him again before looking away.

"Where the hell are they?" Jack was pulling out things from his drawers, searching for his ripped jeans. Sure, he wasn't having a full-blown party anymore, but he still wanted to look nice. Now he glanced at the mirror in front of him. And with Gabe rooting for him…Jack left his thoughts when his mom knocked on his door.

"Come in," he said, looking back at her before continuing his search. She smiled at him and sat down on his bed. "So, how's the new friendship going?"

"It's going well. We're hanging out at Luke's place tomorrow," Jack replied, pulling out the hidden jeans. He tossed it in the white bag with gold writing that sat on his bedroom floor and sat beside his mom.

She pointed at the bag and asked, "What'd you buy?"

Folding his legs pretzel style, Jack responded, "It's a sweater and a watch…and Luke actually bought it as a birthday present."

His mother sighed and rested a hand on his knee. "Look, baby, I'm sure he said it was a gift, but don't let him manipulate you."

"Jesus, Mom, it's just a gift. How's he manipulating me?" Jack scoffed, standing, and leaning against the wall.

"He's buying you expensive things, taking you out, it just seems like—"

"Like what? Like German?" he interrupted. "Or maybe he's someone who actually gives a crap about me?" His mom furrowed her brows and took her time standing. Jack turned away, but she grabbed his face and stared at him.

"You like him, don't you?"

Jack pulled out of her hold and walked over to his bed, muttering, "So what if I do?"

"Jesus, Jack. Do you want a repeat of Middleton High?"

"No! Why would I ever want that?" he shouted back. His mother stared at him with wide eyes, and he huffed, covering his face with his hands. "Of course, I don't…But nothing is going on. We're just friends." He heard his mom huff and the spot beside him on the bed sunk.

She rested her hand on his shoulder and said, "I just don't want you to have to bear that again." Jack nodded and ran his hands down his face.

"I'm gonna go to bed," he muffled. She gave him a sad smile and stood.

"Good night, sweetie." His mom patted his head and made her way out of the room, closing the door behind her. Jack flipped over on his bed and buried his head under his pillow. Of course, he didn't want to be kicked out of another school. His academics couldn't handle that. His heart would find it unbearable.

"Argh!" he groaned.

***

Luke looked at his phone. For the first time in a while, he woke up early on his own. There were no texts from Jack, not that he'd be up this early, but there were about ten texts and two voicemails from Trish. He ignored them, checking his emails instead. The further he stayed away from her, the better off they'd all be.

"Well, good morning," Luke looked up from his phone and smiled.

"Morning, Patricia." She smiled back at him, walking over to the windows.

"So, it's happening again?" she asked, opening the curtains.

Luke sat up and questioned, "What are you talking about?"

"You've been coming home all smiley and watching your phone all day." Patricia pointed out, making her way to the bathroom. "You like someone."

Luke's eyes went wide, and he protested as he walked into the bathroom, "That's not true!"

Patricia stood in the doorway and responded, "I've raised you as if you were my own, Luke. I'm sure I know when you like someone." Luke went to say something, but only sighed heavily and looked from the bathroom mirror to Patricia.

"Okay…okay, so maybe I think I like someone, but it can't be…" Patricia smiled and folded her arms.

"Who is it?"

Luke scratched his forehead and answered, "I think…It might be…" Luke huffed and looked at Patricia. "It might be Jack."

"Well."

Jack stuffed his skateboard into his locker and closed it. Someone tapped him on the shoulder, and he jumped, turning around.

"Jesus, why are you so close?" he exclaimed, walking off.

"Happy birthday," Luke said with a smile, keeping close behind Jack.

"Thanks."

"Ready for tonight?"

"I feel like I should be nervous," Jack joked. Luke chuckled and rested his arm across the other's shoulders. Jack looked up at him and he gulped. He, without a doubt, liked Luke. He slid out of the other's hold, and they walked into class. They made their way over to Gabe who had his arms crossed.

"Way to make me feel like a dumped friend," he grumbled. "Happy birthday, Jack." Jack smiled and thanked him, taking a seat. Luke sat beside Gabe and pat his back.

"You're my friend for life dude. You're fuckin awesome," Luke boasted.

Gabe chuckled. "Well, when ya put it like that."

"You always get here so early," Jack commented, pulling things from his bag.

"Well, unlike King Luke over here," Gabe mocked, receiving a slap on the back of the head. "I don't have my own driver, so I have to drive myself to school."

"Hey, it's not that I can't drive," Luke corrected. "My parents just prefer it if someone else did it."

Jack scoffed and Gabe replied, "Please, I'm your best friend and I know you can't drive."

"Yes, the hell I can."

"You really can't."

"After school, parking lot, I'll drive us to my place," Luke declared.

"Are you sure about this, Gabe?" Jack asked, staring at him. Gabe nodded and he shook Luke's hand. Looked like this would be the last time Jack would see them.

"Alright, boys," the coach shouted. Luke took off his mask and lowered his foil. "Go ahead and get changed, I'll see you all next week." He and his teammates saluted their coach before saluting each other. As he followed the rest of his class to the locker room, he could see Trish standing in the hall. What the hell did she want now? He undressed, then dressed again before grabbing his bag and rushing out of the gym.

"Luke, wait," she called out, but he continued down the hall. The closer he got to the school entrance, the more hastily her heels clicked. "Luke," she whined. He stopped, but he didn't turn to her.

"What do you want, Trish?"

"Are you not gonna look at me?" He huffed and slowly turned. She looked him over before asking, "Are we really over?"

Luke scoffed, "You're asking me that after you tried to kill someone?" She couldn't be serious? He shook his head and went to turn away again.

"So what, you're gay then?"

"I don't know."

"How can you be gay?"

"I don't know, Trish. Maybe I've been gay my whole life and just didn't know it."

"Maybe there's something wrong with you." He could see the tears in her eyes, but his words still stung.

"What century do you think we live in?" he started. "You think just because I dated you, there's no way I could be into guys? That I'm just confused?" He moved in close and searched her eyes. "Look where your delusion's gotten you. You couldn't see past your own fantasies and judged Jack because of the things you've heard." He backed up and gave his final blow. "I may have the blond hair and the blue eyes, but this isn't a fucking fairy tale, and you sure as hell aren't my princess." He shook his head before turning away. "Goodbye, Trish." And with that he left the school building.

"Took you long enough." Jack looked up from his place in the backseat of Gabe's car and smiled. Within the time it took Luke to finish practicing, he changed into his birthday outfit.

"Sorry, had to break up with Trish," Luke huffed, getting into the driver's seat.

"Didn't you do that already?" Jack questioned. Luke nodded, adjusting his mirrors.

"You boys ready?" he asked in the most terrible southern accent his body managed to let out.

Jack reached forward and pat Gabe's shoulder, saying, "I wish you luck." Luke gave him the finger before putting the car into drive. He began swerving, and Gabe grabbed his arm.

"Nope, that's enough driving for you!" Gabe shouted. Luke swerved to the right, making Gabe fly back into his seat. "Gimme back my car!" the other whined. Jack held onto the grab handle and shook his head.

"If you keep driving like this, I'm jumping out," he declared. Luke laughed and sped. They were headed straight for the back of a truck and Gabe and Jack started yelling. Jack squeezed his eyes shut and waited for the impact. But to his surprise, they were slowing down. He peaked out his left eye and instinctively kicked the back of Luke's seat.

"I'm sorry, I had to mess with you guys," Luke chuckled.

Gabe, holding his chest, grumbled, "You are fucking terrible." getting Gabe to yell at him and order him to give his car back. But once he was done playing around, he was, to Gabe and Jack's surprise, a damn good driver.

Once they arrive at Luke's place, thankfully in one piece, Gabe couldn't help but comment, "I had my doubts but you really can drive."

"I told you not to doubt my skills."

Jack got out, following them, and asked, "What exactly are we doing for my birthday other than boosting your ego?"

Luke unlocked the front door and explained, "I figured we have…a kickass birthday party." He opened the door and Jack felt a rush as his fellow classmates greeted him with a 'Happy birthday!' He looked at Luke and the other shook his own hands. "You're amazing. I know!" he told himself. They walked through the crowd of people and Gabe led them straight to the drinks.

"I thought you cancelled it?" Jack pointed out.

Gabe shook his head and clarified, "He cancelled it for Trish." He threw back a shot and went on, "But yelling it in the cafeteria made it very hard to explain to everyone it wasn't actually canceled." He glared at Luke and the other raised his hand for a high five. Gabe rolled his eyes and poured out some more shots. He distributed them between Luke, Jack, and himself. "On the count of three, we drink." Luke smirked and took hold of the glass.

"One," he started. "Two…Three!" He and Gabe tossed back their heads, the alcohol warming their throats.

"What the fuck, man," Gabe exclaimed. Jack looked at him with confusion, then at his shot. "You were supposed to drink it."

Letting off a chuckle, Jack pointed out, "I never agreed though."

Luke began laughing and Gabe took the shot, downing it himself. "Well played, Jack. Well played."

After some more shots, singing, dancing, and slices of cake, Jack and Luke found themselves in the backyard. There were still a few people who'd lingered, but Luke didn't mind. He was too busy staring at Jack.

"Hey." Luke came back into focus and smiled.

"Sorry, what were you saying?" Jack scoffed and sat back in the chair.

"I was thanking you for all this," he looked around before staring straight ahead. "For taking the time to get to know me." He looked at Luke and their eyes met.

Luke's smile was impossible to hide, and he muttered, "No problem." His eyes danced their way down to the floor and soon met with the water swaying in front of them. "Hey," he said, "as my last gift to you, how about I teach you how to swim."

"Sure. I'll take it." Jack went to close his eyes when Luke shot up from his seat.

"Alright, c'mon," he exclaimed, pulling off his shirt.

"What? Now?"

"Yeah, think of it as your first lesson." Luke's jeans dropped and Jack gulped. He still had his boxers on, but Jack could tell all too well what was behind door number one. Not waiting for any more protests, Luke leaned forward and pulled on the other's sweater. "C'mon, I'm not asking you to jump off a cliff. And we can start with simple back floating." Jack stared at Luke, and then his abs. He didn't even bother to look at his boxers again and stood, looking at the ground. He pulled his sweater over his head, kicked his shoes out of the way and lowered his jeans. When he finally took off the t-shirt that he had to pep-talk off his body, he looked at Luke. Putting his hands on his hips, Luke complimented, "Not bad, Jack Whyte, not bad."

"I used to play basketball." Jack watched Luke, taking his time behind him and the other jumped into the six-foot section of the pool.

"That's cool, let's play some time." Luke reached his hand out, but Jack swiped it away.

"I can drown," he complained.

"You don't trust me?" Jack frowned. Of course, he did. He didn't trust *himself* in that goddamn water *with* Luke. "Come on." Jack nodded and he shook his head.

"Alright." He put both feet in before jumping. He was slightly on his tip toes, but he did his best to get to Luke. The other tried to back up and Jack lunged forward, grabbing him. They laughed, but their noses were almost touching. Jack slightly pulled away, but Luke's hand was on his waist. "Okay...Now what?"

"Kick your feet up and I'll hold them." Jack nodded and huffed. He counted to three and kicked up. Luke caught them and began moving in the water. "Focus on floating…Close your eyes and focus. I'm right here." Jack nodded and closed his eyes. The other looked at him and smiled. He continued to float through the water, Luke barely holding him now. Jack could feel the cool weather breeze against his face and listened to Luke's slow breathing. He went to say something when he suddenly felt himself halt in the water. He slowly opened his eyes and Luke was smiling.

"Why'd we stop?" he asked.

"We've reached eight feet."

"What?" Jack threw his legs down and grabbed onto Luke, wrapping his arm around his neck.

"I was gonna let you go, but now I'm glad I didn't." Luke chuckled, resting his hand on the small of Jack's back.

"You're an asshole," the other mumbled. He'd unintentionally pulled Luke closer, and his chin was against the other's shoulder.

"Sure," Luke stretched. They continued to hold each other, Luke doing all of the work to keep them afloat.

"Today…was fun," Jack muffled, his lips now pressed against Luke's shoulder. They were around the five feet section now, making it a lot easier for him to stand. All he received was a nod, before lips touched his shoulder. He didn't say anything and received another kiss on the neck, and then the cheek. Jack slowly turned his head and now they were staring at each other. Luke leaned in, but Jack couldn't wait and filled the gap, overwhelming the water between them. Both hands were on his waist now and he pulled away.

Luke realized what he'd done and apologized, "I'm so sorry…I didn't—" He went to pull away, but Jack pulled him into another kiss. When they parted lips again, Jack stared at Luke.

"It's okay," he reassured. Luke smiled and he leaned in for another. Jack opened his mouth, feeling Luke's tongue intrude. He ran his hands up the back of Luke's neck and into his hair. Jack went to pull away again when he heard Gabe.

"Holy shit!" he yelled. Luke huffed, pulling away from Jack. He'd completely forgotten there were still people at the house. Jack hid his face and began walking to the shallow end of the pool. "You guys started hooking up…without me?" Gabe slurred, pushing out his bottom lip. Luke pulled himself up out of the pool and pat his friend's shoulder. Jack met them, standing beside Luke.

"You can stay in the guest room," Luke suggested. "There's no way I'm letting you drive." He ushered Gabe into the house and looked around. "Patricia," he called out. Patricia looked at him and smiled.

"What is it, dear?"

"Can you just make sure everyone gets home safely," he started. "Jack and Gabe are gonna stay the night."

"Of course, Luke." Patricia looked between the three boys before saying, "Good night." They all did their best to respond before Jack and Luke worked together to carry Gabe up the stairs.

"I'm happy…for you guys," he mumbled. Jack and Luke looked at each other and couldn't help but smile. "I knew…you licked each other." Jack laughed and patted Gabe's shoulder.

"Yeah, we licked each other," he mocked.

"I said liked, goddammit." Luke couldn't hold it in anymore and he started laughing. When they reached the guest bedroom, they removed Gabe's shoes and clothes, lying him down on the bed.

"Good night, buddy," Luke said softly, patting Gabe's head. The other nodded and cuddled up to the pillow he rested his head on. Luke and Jack tip toed out of the room and Jack turned to Luke.

"Where's the other guest—" He was cut off by the other's lips again and he sighed. Luke pushed him against the nearest wall and received a groan.

He slightly pulled away and stared at Jack's lips, asking, "Is it weird that I wanna have sex with you, right now?" Did he really just ask if…Jack let his heart panic, but his brain managed to pull off a smirk.

"I don't think so," he muttered. Luke nodded and he kissed Jack again, holding his hips close. Jack was a bit shocked, but as they pressed against each other, it made sense why Luke had suddenly asked him that question. The organ between his legs was rock hard. Jack kissed Luke one more time before letting the other pull him along.

"Welcome to my den," Luke announced, turning the lights on just enough for them to see each other. The bedroom had to be at least twice the size of Jack's. And not only was there a king-sized bed in the middle of the room, but Luke had two large lounge chairs, a mounted flat screen, a desk – "Hey," Luke muttered, getting Jack's attention.

"Sorry," he replied. "I don't know why I didn't expect your room to be as extra as the rest of your house." Luke chuckled and he tugged on the other's hand. Jack fell into the kiss, feeling Luke's arms around his waist. His feet began moving forward and before he knew it, he was lying on top of Luke. He sat up and they smiled at one another. Luke went to sit up when he huffed, feeling himself rub against Jack. "H-Hold on," the other stuttered. Jack got up and pulled off his boxers, Luke quickly doing the same in his spot on the bed. Jack's eyes scanned his body, making Luke turn red.

"U-Um…" Jack snapped out of his thoughts, and he sat down on the bed, scooting up until he was about in the middle. Luke looked at him and crouched on the bed. Jack planted his feet, squeezing his legs together and Luke chuckled. "How am I supposed to kiss you?" Jack shrugged and his eyes went wide as Luke put his hands on his knees.

"W-Wait," he stuttered, but Luke was already kneeling between his legs. His eyes fluttered and his partner took a deep breath as their hard-ons touched again. Luke leaned forward and their lips met. He rested his arms above Jack's head, slowly working his way down from his lips to his neck. "D-Do you know what you're doing?" a question Jack should've asked before they got this far. His eyes met with Luke's as the other licked down his chest and he felt a shiver down his spine. It was really happening.

"I think I have a sense," the other muttered, smirking soon after. Jack bit his lip and lied his head back. He felt Luke's tongue pass his nipples and his breath hitched, giving Luke the indication that he was doing a good job. He let his fingers work on the other's nipples while he moved down. "Jack," he muffled, lips now sitting at the other's v-line.

"Yeah." Jack sighed, slightly sitting up to see his face.

"I uh…I never sucked another guy's dick before," he confessed, something Jack expected.

"W-We can switch places," Jack suggested.

Luke waved his hand in the air and declared, "I've watched enough porn. I think I got it," And with that, he looked back down at the erection in front of him. He took hold of it and Jack groaned. Luke was holding his cock a bit tight, but it felt good. The other gulped before lowering his mouth down on Jack. He received a gasp and he pulled away. "Holy shit," he exclaimed, letting go of Jack.

"Wh-Why'd you stop?" Jack questioned. "It felt good." Luke blushed and sat up, waving his hands. Jack sat up too and stared at him.

"I th-think it's just too weird for me," he said, sitting down. His lower half knew he didn't want to stop, but he just couldn't bring himself to do it. He felt Jack's hand on his shoulder, and it slid down his chest.

"I'll do it for you then," he offered, now running his finger across the other's tip. Luke closed his eyes and nodded.

"B-But…what about you?" Jack ignored his question and took him in his mouth, kneeling on the bed. "Ho…shit." Luke put one hand on the bed to hold himself up, the other attached to Jack's hair. Jack licked up the side, before using his lips to nibble on the skin.

"Jack." Luke breathed, looking down at him. Jack put the head in his mouth, and his tongue whirled around it, making Luke grip his hair tighter. "H-Have you…done this…before?" He suddenly felt the need to be Jack's first. He *wanted* to be his first. Jack let the other leave his mouth with a 'pop' and he sat on his lap, sighing as their cocks rubbed together.

Jack took hold of both their erections, and rested his head on Luke's shoulder, explaining, "It's...my first time too...I've only practiced...with dildos." Luke felt himself shiver from the shy words and he grabbed Jack's hand, which had been vigorously moving up and down. "What?" Jack sat up and looked at Luke.

"I-I wanna...make you feel good too."

"But I do." Jack chuckled, knowing all too well what Luke was implying. Suddenly, he was flipped onto his back and he moaned, Luke's fingers against his entrance.

"I mean...here." Jack stared at him before nodding. Luke smiled and kissed Jack before sliding off the bed. While he searched his dresser for condoms and lube, Jack was having a slight panic attack. Yes, he wanted to have sex. It'd finally be over with, and it'd be with someone who genuinely cared about him. Now Jack covered his face. But what if it didn't feel good ...He'd been practicing but what if the real deal hurt more? As he drowned in his thoughts, Luke was climbing back on the bed, placing the lube and condom close by. "Hey," he whispered. Jack looked at him and gulped. "Ready?"

Jack took a deep breath and looked down. While Luke had easier access to this than the sexual parts he'd dealt with in the past, they reacted the same. Jack threw his head back as he felt Luke probing his entrance. He'd done it a million times to himself, but feeling someone else's fingers asking for entry was so much more exciting. Luke pushed his index finger in, and he could feel the other's warmth around him. Just the thought alone of him being inside Jack in the next few minutes made him twitch between his legs, but he had to control himself. "P-Put in another." Jack breathed, clutching the sheets. Luke saw this and he grabbed the other's hands, putting them over his head. Their eyes met and Jack lifted his head, kissing Luke. As their tongues fought, Luke pushed in his middle finger, the digit joining in the warmth.

"Feel good?" he teased, Jack moaning against his lips. Jack nodded and he raised his hips, rubbing their bodies together.

"One…m-more," he stuttered, his body craving to be filled. Luke pulled his fingers out achingly slow, getting Jack to twitch against them. He pressed his index, middle, and ring fingers together and slowly pushed them into Jack. "Hngh…fuck," he groaned. His hips were completely off the bed now and Luke grabbed one, pushing him back down. "Luke." The other nodded and his fingers quickly moved back and forth. "I-I'm…I'm gonna—" He bit his lip, but his orgasm was halted by Luke's hand around his cock. He glanced up and the other looked at him with furrowed brows.

"Wait," Luke ordered. Jack's eyes rolled back as his fingers came out and he lied there, panting; waiting. Luke ripped open the condom wrapper and worked it onto his cock. He didn't waste any time and lined himself up at Jack's entrance. He lied against Jack, letting him wrap his arms around his neck, and began pushing into the other. Luke exhaled the air that he'd held for some reason and looked at Jack. "Y-You okay?" Jack only nodded and he threw his head back.

"D-Deeper," he breathed.

"H-How? Y-You're too tight." Jack huffed and pushed Luke away. "Wh-What?"

"L-Lie down…" Jack began sitting up, Luke slipping out of him. "I'm…I'm gonna get on top." Luke was sure he came in the condom after that, but he didn't look down. Instead, he did as he was told and lied back. "Hmph," Jack moaned through gritted teeth. He moved back and forth on Luke's cock before grabbing it with his hand. He put his other hand on the other's chest, and slowly sat down.

"Wow." Luke sighed, resting a hand on Jack's ass. Jack nodded and raised his hips again. When he was finally used to Luke, he put both hands above the other's head and felt hands grip his ass.

"I-I'm coming…faster," he moaned, now leaning on his forearms. Luke didn't know how, but he raised his hips from the bed and thrusted up, making Jack shout a moan.

"F-Fuck." He could feel Jack squeeze against him, and he came in the condom. Jack reached down between them and held his cock as he started coming too. He huffed and pressed their foreheads together. He moved his hips high enough so that Luke could come out, and once he was, they both groaned and kissed.

"W-We should…" Jack panted. And somehow, Luke knew what he meant. He sat up, holding Jack's waist. Jack smiled at him and rested his head on his shoulder, arms wrapped around his neck. Luke tried to catch his breath before standing and making his way to the bathroom.

Part 4

Patricia hummed as she made her way up the stairs to Luke's room. Gabe had gotten up early so she got him settled, but she wasn't sure which guest room Jack had slept in. She opened Luke's bedroom door and smiled.

"Luke, it's time to…" As she walked into the room, she spotted Jack. Luke, hearing Patricia, slowly sat up and looked at her. "Breakfast is ready," she whispered.

"Thank you," Luke whispered back, rubbing his eyes. Patricia nodded and left, closing the door behind her. Now he looked down at Jack and moved the hair out of his face. "Jack, wake up."

Jack shuffled and asked, "Is it time to leave already?"

Luke leaned in and kissed Jack's cheek, responding, "We've got about an hour to get ready." Jack nodded, but as he went to drift back to sleep, he realized he wasn't lying on his ten-year-old mattress and he sure as hell wasn't alone. He sat up and looked at Luke, eyes wide. "Good morning," the other greeted, smiling.

Jack stared at him and questioned, "D-Did we…Did you…Were we…"

Luke chuckled and answered, "Yeah, we got a little carried away last night and went all the way." He moved a bit closer and reached out for Jack's hand. Jack found himself not moving away. "It was…great…and I don't want that to be the end."

"Y-You're kidding," Jack said, still staring at Luke. The other shook his head. "Fuck," he breathed. He pulled his hand away and stood. Jack ran his fingers through his hair and began pacing.

"Hey," Luke called out, getting up from the bed. Jack looked at him and gulped. He let Luke hold his waist and they stared into each other's eyes. "You alright?" Jack sighed and nodded, resting his forehead against the other's. Luke wasn't German. Not even close. He was so much better.

"I can't believe we had sex," he managed to chuckle.

"Yeah," Luke muttered. Jack looked at him and he pulled the other close. They kissed and Luke huffed. "We should probably get ready for school." Jack nodded and followed behind Luke to the bathroom.

After they got dressed, Jack and Luke headed downstairs, to the dining room.

"Morning," Gabe cheerfully greeted. Jack took a seat across from him at the dining table and raised his brow.

Taking a seat beside Jack, Luke questioned, "What are you still doing here?"

"I figured we'd all leave together." Luke stared at Gabe before nodding. They ate breakfast, but there was an overbearing silence, and Jack had enough.

"So, the party was good," he muttered, moving the eggs on his plate.

Gabe smirked and he sat back in his seat, pointing out, "You two kissed in the pool."

Luke nodded and replied, "We did." Now Gabe leaned in and looked at Jack, grinning.

Jack looked up and furrowed his brows. "Wh-What?"

"You guys totally banged." Shit. Did he hear them? Jack gulped and sat up.

"I don't know…what you're talking about," he responded, looking away.

Luke looked at Jack in shock and joked, "Are you ashamed of me?" Jack's head turned so quickly he almost gave himself whiplash. "What? He would've found out anyway," Luke mumbled, going back to his breakfast. Jack stared at him before taking a deep breath and returning to his food.

Gabe, too excited to hide his smile, asked, "So are you guys gonna date? Or are you just gonna be fuck buddies?" Jack nearly choked on his orange juice, and he had to sit back in his seat.

"I-I don't know." He coughed. He looked at Luke and the other was smiling.

He didn't look at Jack, but Luke said, "It's whatever you want."

"Do I have a choice?"

"Maybe? Maybe not?" Gabe looked between the two, enjoying the show in front of him.

"I guess we'll find out at school."

Gabe threw his hands in the air and exclaimed, "I need a sequel! Why are you guys teasing me like this?"

Before either of them could reply, Patricia walked in and announced, "Boys, Ralph is here." Luke sighed and stood, patting Jack's shoulder. He followed behind him, Gabe gulping down his orange juice before running after them. As they got outside and close to the car, Jack's phone began to ring.

"Morning, Mom," he greeted.

"Are you on your way to school?" she asked.

"Yep, I'm coming home after."

"Alright, be safe, sweetie."

"I will, Mom." He hung up the phone and felt Luke's eyes on him as he got in the car. "What?"

"Your parents are so nice to you," he pointed out, moving over as Gabe got in and closed the door.

"Yeah, aren't yours?"

Luke shrugged and explained, "I don't really see my parents that often. I would consider Patricia more of a parent than my mom and dad."

"But don't you see your dad at school?" Jack questioned. Luke scoffed and folded his arms.

"Have you ever seen my dad at school?"

"Not really."

"Exactly. He's always in his office. Sure, when I first started going there, he'd come to my matches but now I just know him as Vice Principal Finnegan." He huffed and continued. "My mom is okay. I mean, she supports me when she can and when my dad is being an asshole about everything."

Gabe shrugged and added, "Dude, be thankful you've got three parents now! I haven't seen my parents in years because of their jobs."

"You live by yourself?" Jack questioned.

"Nah, my older brother lives with me."

"Oh." Jack sighed and concluded, "Gabe's right though, sure your dad can be an asshole sometimes, but you've got two moms and a guy who'll cheer you on once and a while."

"Yeah, I guess you're right," Luke said with a smile.

"We're here, you little rug rats," Ralph announced, as he parked in front of the school.

"And let's not forget about the one and only, Ralph," Gabe complimented.

Ralph rolled his eyes, a smile on his face and said, "Yeah, yeah."

As they got out the car, Luke exclaimed, "See you this afternoon." Ralph waved at them and drove off. "You wanna get pizza later?" Luke asked, looking at Jack.

"What?" Gabe groaned. "Why're you always doing something when I have swim meet?"

"Sorry." Luke chuckled, opening the school's doors.

Jack nodded and replied, "Yeah, let's go." Gabe looked between them before smirking.

"Oh, I see. You guys are going on a date."

Luke shrugged. "I mean, if that's what Jack wants."

Jack scowled at him before saying, "I like how I'm given the option to run now." Luke laughed and they walked to their lockers.

"Are we gonna sit together at lunch?" Gabe asked, rummaging through his locker.

Jack smiled and responded, "Yeah, I'll sit with you guys today." He heard Luke's locker close and then arms wrapped around his waist. "So, I guess I didn't have a choice," he breathed, still smiling. He closed his locker, turned to Luke, and their noses were almost touching.

"Just one kiss," Luke whispered, looking down at the other's lips. Jack looked around before giving Luke a peck on the lips. He turned and tried to walk away, but Luke pulled him back. "Nope, not satisfying enough." Jack rolled his eyes and let the other kiss him. He rested his hand in Luke's hair, letting his tongue explore his mouth.

"Okay, lovebirds, let's go to class, yeah?" Gabriel said, hoping they'd stop. Luke pulled away and smirked at Jack. He rested his arm across the other's shoulders and Jack shook his head.

"Oh my God, are they going out?"

"No, Luke's not into guys."

"Didn't he just break up with Trish?"

Luke couldn't help but chuckle and he and Jack walked into the classroom. As he took his seat, he realized Trish wasn't there. He looked at her seat for a while, before reaching into his bag for a pen and paper.

At lunch, Jack sat with Gabe and Luke as promised. And of course, they were surrounded by some of their classmates.

"Are you guys really together?" a girl questioned, staring between them. Luke looked at Gabe and then at Jack, whose face was buried in his book.

"Hey," he whispered. Jack looked at him and he leaned in to kiss the other.

"Holy shit." Everyone began mumbling to each other at the table. Jack buried his face back in his book and although he looked like he didn't care, he was dancing on daisies.

Luke sighed and declared, "Jack and I are dating."

"I hooked them up," Gabe pointed out, wanting some credit.

"Sure you did," Jack commented, leaning against Luke's arm. Luke looked down at the other and tried to kiss him again, only to be pushed away.

"Damn I'm good. I made a perfect match," Gabe exclaimed, faking tears. Suddenly, a girl pushed through the group of teens and sat across from Luke.

Luke asked, "I thought you didn't come today?"

Trish rolled her eyes and said, "I couldn't bear to see your fucking face so early in the morning."

"Why the hell are you sitting here now?" Gabe interjected.

Trish looked at him before looking back at Luke. "You know, it's funny how I had to warm up to Gabriel and all your 'friends' just to fit in. I even had to sit and tolerate that thing you call a sport. And all this little prick had to do was nearly drown and now everyone loves him. Isn't that funny, Luke?"

Luke only smiled and replied, "You do realize that you're the only one who didn't take the time to get to know Jack, right?"

She ignored Luke and looked at Jack. "Well, look at you. You nearly die, he saves you, and now you're his boyfriend. He must have fucked you good."

Gabriel, annoyed, responded, "What the fuck is wrong with you? You got dumped, get over it."

"Who the hell asked you?"

"Jesus, what is wrong with you?" Jack suddenly questioned, slamming his book down. "I didn't just come out of nowhere and 'seduce' Luke if that's what you're implying. You made the decision to put your heart over your mind, you didn't think before you acted, and you lost a boyfriend in the process. That's got nothing to do with me." She stared at him; her jaw dropped.

"You're a fucking dick and all you want is money."

"If that's all I wanted, don't you think I would've stayed at my old school?" Their audience had been making oooos and ohs as they went back and forth. Having enough, Trish got up and stormed out of the cafeteria. It was silent for a bit until someone started whispering and it became loud once again.

"Wow, you really didn't hold back there," Luke commented, staring at Jack.

"She was getting on my fucking nerves," Jack huffed. "I just wanna read." Luke chuckled and nodded, and he let the other lean up against him again while he tried looking for a conversation to join.

"Thanks," Luke said, grabbing the pizza from the counter. He walked over to Jack and sat down, passing him a slice.

"Trish really lost it today," Jack huffed, taking a bite.

Luke nodded and replied, "We were good while we lasted." He shook his head. "I could only imagine the shit I would have to deal with if that relationship went any further."

Jack nodded back and pointed out, "You really thought with your dick with that one." Luke chuckled and he raised his brow.

"So you're saying I chose right this time?" Jack held in a laugh while he ate and shook his head.

"That's not what I'm saying." He chuckled watching the other before his eyes dropped to his plate.

"Can I uh, ask you something?" Luke had to know.

Jack furrowed his brows and responded, "What's up?"

"Why'd you really get kicked out of Middleton?" the other asked, looking up at Jack.

Jack looked down at his pizza and huffed, "I guess I never told you the whole story."

Luke shrugged and muffled, "I mean…if it's something you'd rather not talk about…I won't bother you about it anymore."

Jack sat back in his seat and took another bite of his pizza before he started. "No, it's okay…I started dating this rich guy during my 11th year. You think you spoiled me this week?" He scoffed. "This guy tried buying me a car." He sighed now. "We'd been going out for about three months, just around winter break, but I still wasn't ready to have sex…He kept trying to pin me down and force himself on me. So, I punched him in the nose." Jack chuckled and looked at Luke. "I broke it, and the maid heard him yell like a baby, and came running up. He told her to call the police. Of course, everyone took his side, and I was kicked out." Now he shrugged. "My friends weren't even real friends. I realized that they were only close to me so that they could be close with him." He rolled his eyes and took another bite of his pizza.

"So…if you don't mind me asking, why'd you let me go so far?"

Jack shrugged again and answered, "I would say the alcohol but that's a terrible joke for right now." He ate the last piece of pizza and wiped his mouth. "I guess it was because you actually asked me. He never once bothered to see if I was okay with it, he just assumed because we were dating that I'd be down to have sex." Now he smiled. "Yesterday…was weird…but I felt safe, like I could trust you, and so I was okay with you being my first."

Luke was blushing and asked his last embarrassing question, "Was…Was it any good?" Jack gawked at him before covering his mouth, trying to hold in his laughs.

"I thought I made it pretty clear." Luke was even more red than before and he nodded, looking away.

"I'm telling you, I can do it," Luke exclaimed. He and Jack were in the hallway of his house, skateboarding.

Jack covered his face but peaked between his fingers, muffling, "You're definitely going to hurt yourself." Luke got on the skateboard and started moving across the hall.

"See," he said, continuing to move. He tried to turn, but his foot fell off, and he went flying, trying to grab Jack. The other caught him and swung around, planting his feet to keep his balance. Luke chuckled and looked at Jack. "A little more practice and I'll get the hang of it." Jack shook his head and they kissed. Luke stood up straight and held Jack's waist.

"I hope you boys are being careful," Patricia called out. "Dinner will be ready soon."

"Okay!" they replied back. Luke looked at Jack and smiled.

"Wanna go up to my room for a bit?" he asked.

"Are you trying to do a quickie before dinner?" Luke leaned in and kissed Jack's ear.

"Maybe." Jack went to kiss Luke when the front door opened.

"Luke Finnegan!" Luke turned his head and he gulped. His father was rushing toward him. "Step away from that boy."

Jack stepped back and apologized, "S-Sorry Mr. Finnegan, I—"

"Get out of my house immediately."

"Dad, you're overreacting," Luke scoffed.

"I told you not to associate yourself with him."

Luke's mother put her hand on her husband's shoulder and pointed out, "But they seem to be getting along. I don't see the problem."

"I'll just leave," Jack declared. He went to walk to his skateboard and Luke grabbed his hand.

"No, you won't!" Luke protested. Luke's father grabbed both their hands and pulled them apart.

"Enough!" he yelled.

"William, stop!" Luke's mother shouted, pulling him back. "You know Jack hasn't done anything wrong! The Williams used their money to get him kicked out of Middleton." She looked at Jack. "Have you ever thought to hear his side? Are you going to let gossip and money blind your judgement?" Luke's father stared between the two boys before looking at his wife. He let go of their wrists. Mr. Finnegan walked back to their suitcases following their butler up the stairs. Luke's mother looked between the two boys and smiled. "Please, Jack, stay for dinner." Jack looked at Luke and the other took his hand again.

"Okay."

"Great," Luke's mother sighed, looking back at them. "I'll just freshen up. You can head to the dining room." Luke nodded and Jack could feel him squeeze his hand.

"You sure you want to stay?" he asked. "We can go out to eat."

Jack pouted and nodded. "It's okay. Patricia already cooked for us so we might as well eat here." Luke stared into the other's eyes before sighing. Jack smiled as the other pulled him along to the dining room.

Taking a seat, Luke placed his napkin on his lap and looked over the spread on the table. "Help yourself," he muttered, reaching for the bowl of mashed potatoes. Jack watched his boyfriend gently place the white fluff of carbs on his plate before placing the bowl back on the table. Luke glanced at him, raising the fork stacked with slices of chicken above its serving plate. "What?"

Jack quickly shook his head and reached out for the bowl of garlic green beans. "Nothing…I've just never seen you like…this."

"And what is this?"

"Proper. Quiet," Jack tried to explain. Luke chuckled.

"Is that a bad thing?" he muffled, stuffing a spoon of mash into his mouth. Jack couldn't help but smirk and he shrugged.

"Not at all." The room was filled with their utensils hitting their plates and for a moment, they enjoyed each other's company in the silence.

"Jesus, can you just give him a chance," a voice from down the hall attempted to whisper as it approached the dining room. Jack looked up and watched as Mr. and Ms.

Finnegan walked in. "How's dinner so far?" she questioned, sitting in front of Jack.

The other smiled, making sure to clear his throat before answering, "Pretty good." Ms. Finnegan smiled and soon the room was filled with clinking again. "How long have you two been together?" Luke's mother asked, cutting her steak.

"Mom," Luke groaned, covering his face.

Jack smirked and answered, "It's only been a day."

"Oh wow, so you are in the honeymoon stage," she teased. Jack chuckled, but Luke was still dying from embarrassment.

"I guess you could say that."

"So, are you and Trish no more?"

Luke nodded and replied, "It was toxic." His mother nodded and continued eating.

"What are you going to be studying Jack," Luke's father suddenly asked. Both teens looked at him and Jack gulped. He could tell Mr. Finnegan wasn't impressed and his answer probably wouldn't make things better.

"I'm planning to study architecture and engineering."

"That's amazing!" Ms. Finnegan exclaimed.

"I wanted to be an architect when I was a little younger than you two," Mr. Finnegan confessed, the attention back on him.

Luke questioned, "Why didn't you?"

"Oh, I did, but then I realized in my first year that it just wasn't for me, so I took up educational studies."

"Richard was a professor at MZU for a couple years before he went to Thomas Pry," Ms. Finnegan boasted.

"And since Luke wants to study law, it may as well be a full ride for him."

"You want to study law?" Jack asked, looking at Luke.

He nodded and pointed out, "I was on the debate team in primary school and halfway through secondary school and I've just always been interested in law." Now he smirked and joked, "I also think I'm pretty good at convincing people." Jack rolled his eyes and continued eating his food.

"I'm sorry you had to endure that," Luke huffed. Jack smiled and kissed him. They were standing outside, waiting for Jack's taxi to arrive.

"Your dad really loves you," he pointed out.

"What?"

"He was literally about to fight me to protect you from whatever nonsense the Williams filled his head with." Luke scoffed before shrugging.

"I guess so." He pulled Jack close and rested his head on the other's shoulder. "I'm just happy he seems to like you." Now he kissed his neck. "I really like you."

Jack ran his fingers through Luke's hair and chuckled. "I like you too."

Part 5

Jack huffed as he walked to the cafeteria. He was a couple months into the spring semester and Luke and Gabe had been acting weird all week. He'd already been dealing with the stress from applying for graduation, opening acceptance/rejection letters and now he had to deal with them. When he walked into the cafeteria, everyone was gathered by the window. He stared at them, watching their heads turn as he walked pass. Jack was about to sit down when Gabe popped up in front of him.

"Hey," he exclaimed.

"Shit." Jack sighed, stepping back. He made his way to a seat, asking, "What the hell's going on?"

Gabe grabbed his arm, pulling him along and said, "Coming through, make room." They moved through the crowd and stood at the window. "Okay, look up." Jack furrowed his brows and looked up at the sky.

"Holy shit," he muttered. In the sky, a small plane began shooting out smoke and as each word came out, Jack felt his stomach sink further and further.

Jack! Will you go to prom with me? – Luke

"Well?" Jack turned around and he spotted Luke standing on one of the lunchroom tables. The crowd of students split down the middle, allowing Jack to walk by. As he walked toward Luke, the other jumped down from the table, smiling at him. When they reached each other, Jack hit his arm with his book.

"Why do you always have to be so dramatic?" he questioned. Luke smirked and kissed him.

"So, is that a yes?" he asked. Jack scowled at him before nodding.

"I guess so." The crowd of students cheered for them, and Luke gave Jack another kiss. Gabe came over to his friends and rested his arm across their shoulders.

"Congratulations, guys," he said. "Should I start passing out the wedding invitations?" Jack hit him in the stomach with his book and they sat down.

"You're so extra sometimes," Jack pointed out, opening his book. Luke rested his arm on the other's waist and kissed him on the cheek.

"Because I can be," he responded bluntly.

"Well, I don't have a date. So, can we all wear the same color?" Gabe questioned. Luke and Jack looked at him before scoffing.

"Gabe, that's not how it works," Jack said behind his book.

"Come on," he whined. Luke ignored him and looked at Jack.

"What color tie should we wear?"

"Uh...I don't know. Blue?"

"I'll buy purple then." Jack chuckled and rolled his eyes, continuing to read.

"Do you want to throw a prom after party at the house?" Luke's mom asked. They sat at the dinner table, his mother making small talk as usual.

"No, I'm thinking of going somewhere with Jack afterwards," Luke answered.

"Well, if you need anything, just let us know. It's good to see you so happy." Luke nodded and continued eating.

"If you need to borrow the cars or estate, just let me know," his father muttered. Luke looked up at him and he smiled.

"Thanks, Dad."

His father looked up from his plate and gave him a small smile. "Of course."

Jack hummed as he walked back into his room from the bathroom. He sat down at his desk and looked at his phone.

1 missed facetime from Luke
Hey, what u upto?

He clicked on the missed call and waited for the dial tone. "Hey, you called earlier?" Jack asked, looking up at his phone. Luke had no shirt on, and he looked like he was getting ready for bed.

"Yeah, I was gonna ask if you wanted to go suit shopping this weekend?"

"Sure, we can invite Gabe," Jack suggested, looking back at his homework.

"I suppose. I won't hear the end of it if we don't."

"True." Luke pulled on his pajama pants and huffed, staring at Jack.

"Hey, um…I don't know if you heard, but I have another match coming up next week."

"Yeah, it's against Middleton, right?"

"You're not worried about seeing your crazy ex again?" Jack scoffed and shook his head.

"Why would I be? I don't even know if he still plays," Jack replied. Luke stared at him before shrugging.

"As long as you're not worried, I won't be."

Jack nodded and ordered, "And even if he is there, just ignore him. He's a cocky prick."

"Yes, sir." Luke plopped down on his bed and huffed. "So, what you doin'?"

"Homework? Something you should probably be doing as well."

"Eh, I rather look at my boyfriend's cute face." Jack rolled his eyes and he looked at Luke. He could hear shifting on the bed and he smirked.

"Are you doing something weird?" Luke looked around the room and pouted.

"I don't know what you mean."

Jack shook his head and responded, "I'm gonna finish my homework so you should probably hang up. I'll see you tomorrow." Luke frowned, but he smiled when Jack smiled at him.

"See you tomorrow." Jack nodded and the other hung up the phone.

"God, why do you always choose somewhere so expensive?" Jack mumbled as he looked at the suits in front of him. He, along with Gabe and Luke met at the mall and were at their third suit store.

Luke ignored his boyfriend and started looking at suits for himself. "Stop complaining, you're my date so I'm buying your suit."

"I know, but just once, I'd like to do something that doesn't cost so much money."

Luke wrapped his arms around Jack's waist and pointed out, "That's what the pizza shop is for." Jack scoffed and continued looking through the over-priced suits. "I promise, I'll think of something."

Jack looked back at Luke and said, "Promise?"

"Promise, babe." Jack smiled and kissed him.

"Can you do something else for me too?" he muttered against his lips.

"What?" Jack leaned back, looking at Luke.

"Wear your hair down like this more often." He reached up and ran his hand over the blonde strands laying against Luke's forehead. "I like it like this." Luke bit his lip and squeezed Jack's waist.

"You got it."

"Could you guys just look for suits and stop touching each other for just a few seconds," Gabe complained, walking past the couple. Luke playfully pushed Gabe and he chuckled.

"Luke, this one would look pretty good on you," Jack exclaimed, Luke letting him go. The suit was jet black with a velvet trim. Jack pulled it from the rack and looked at the price tag. "Okay, maybe not."

"What? What's the price?" Luke questioned, taking the tag out of the other's hand. "That's not bad at all."

Jack rolled his eyes and replied sarcastically, "Yeah, a suit that's nearly a thousand dollars is not bad." Luke looked at the size and nodded.

"I'm gonna buy it," he concluded, walking over to the register and placing the suit on it. As he made his way back to Jack's side, he grabbed a suit that caught his eye. Pressing it against the other's chest, he pointed out, "This would look good on you." Jack looked down at the suit and shrugged. It was a black suit with a leather trim.

"Can I just wear some suspenders and a button up shirt?" Jack responded.

Luke pinched Jack's cheek and declared, "You're wearing a suit." Jack pouted and sluggishly followed Luke. The other picked up two royal blue ties before walking to the register.

"Would you like a fitting, sir?" the cashier questioned. Luke nodded and she began ringing up the suits. "Would you like to do it today or schedule a date?"

Luke looked at Jack before replying, "Let's do it today."

"That will be two thousand, one hundred and nine dollars and five cents." Jack huffed and rested his chin on his boyfriend's shoulder, watching as Luke took out his black card.

"I swear, one day, that thing is going to stop working," Jack mumbled. Luke looked back at him with a smile before turning to the cashier again. She took the suits and walked around the counter.

"I will go ahead and hand these to the tailor. You are free to come and grab me when you are ready for your fitting."

"Thank you." Luke stepped to the side and looked at Gabe who was purchasing his suit. "You're not gonna get fitted?"

Gabe shook his head and replied, "Nah, it's not necessary." Jack walked over to him and looked at the price on the register. Gabe's suit was black with velvet, vintage print on the trim. He walked back over to Luke and hit his arm.

"Ow, what?"

Jack inquires, "Why can't you spend six hundred on a suit? Why do you always have to buy such expensive shit?"

Luke now grabbed Jack's waist and answered, "I always like to look good for the person I'm with."

Gabriel shouted, "What's that supposed to mean? You tryna say I have no one to look good for?"

Luke chuckled. "Nope." Gabe hit him before smiling.

After finishing their fittings and dropping Gabe off, Ralph dropped Luke and Jack at the Finnegan residence. The couple walked into the house and Patricia greeted them. They made their way to Luke's room, hanging up their garment bags. Luke lied down first, taking off his jacket and tossing it on the couch beside his bed. Jack removed his shoes, rolling up his sleeves and sitting on the bed.

"Does your mom know you're staying over tonight?" Luke questioned, wrapping his arms around Jack's waist, and pulling him to lie down.

Jack shook his head and placed his phone on the end table. "I told her that I'd call her when I'm on my way home." Luke now sat up and hovered over Jack.

"So, you're not staying?"

"No, I've got homework." Jack moved his legs so that Luke could kneel between them.

"So mean," Luke mumbled, leaning in for a kiss. "How long has it been since we last did *it*?" he suddenly asked.

Jack shrugged and replied, "I don't know, do I look like I keep count?"

Luke leaned down and bit Jack's ear, whispering, "Yeah." He looked at Jack, searching his eyes, before kissing him. Jack wrapped his arms around Luke's neck and pulled him closer, feeling their lower halves touch. Luke groaned in his boyfriend's mouth and held Jack's hip with his left hand, his other hand resting beside the brunet's hair.

Jack broke the kiss and suddenly questioned, "D-Do you keep count?" Luke smirked and started licking at Jack's neck.

"Yeah." He huffed against a hickey that he left on the boy a few days back.

"Well…How many t-times?"

"Over the last few months, this is our thirty-third time."

"The fact that you keep count is so fucking creepy." Why was he so weird?

"Sorry, I couldn't help it."

"Okay, no more talking." Jack lifted Luke's head and kissed him. Luke pulled Jack closer by the waist and put his hands under the other's shirt. He ran his hand across the other's chest, receiving little whimpers within their kiss.

Jack began unbuckling Luke's pants when the door slowly opened and a woman spoke, "Luke, darling, I was wondering if you…" Luke looked up and saw his mother. He stood and she quickly closed the door. "I-If you boys are hungry, dinner is ready."

Luke chuckled and looked back at Jack. "Alright, Mom. Thanks," he called out. He lied back on the bed and kissed Jack. "Sorry about that," he whispered against the other's lips.

Jack gave Luke a smile before muttering, "No worries." Luke sighed and kissed Jack one last time before pulling him into a hug.

"Guess we can just lie here before heading downstairs," Luke said.

Jack chuckled and agreed, "Yeah…looks like we're back to thirty-two times huh." Luke let off a small laugh before pulling Jack closer by the waist and kissing him.

"I just made that up. Every time with you feels like our first." Jack smiled and kissed Luke on the neck.

"I can't tell if that's a good thing, but you say the cheesiest shit in the world."

"Only for you, Jack, only for you."

"Are you ready for your match?" Gabe asked Luke. It was the day of Thomas Pry's match against Middleton.

"Yep," he replied, changing into his button up shirt. "Jack told me not to worry so I'm not going to."

"If the boyfriend says not to worry, there's no need to." They finished getting changed before heading out of the gym.

"Well, well," Luke looked up and furrowed his brows. "If it isn't the Thomas Pry Fencing King." Luke stared at the guys across from him before smiling.

"You must be German," he responded.

"Ah, so you've heard," German greeted. "Ready to get your ass kicked tonight?" Luke scoffed and turned away.

"We'll see how good you are." German smirked and nodded before shoving past Gabe and Luke. Luke took a deep breath and Gabe pat his shoulder.

"Don't let him get to you man. He's just doing that on purpose."

Luke put his head back and groaned. "I know." The friends continued down the hall towards the school's entrance, stopping when they spotted Jack.

The other smiled as he saw Luke and walked up to him. Resting his arms across Luke's shoulders, Jack asked, "What's with the face?" He leaned in and kissed him, finally feeling his boyfriend's hands on his waist. "Did you miss me that much?" Luke shook his head and pouted.

"We just ran into your ex," Gabe pointed out. Jack furrowed his brows and leaned back to look at Luke and Gabe.

"They're already here? What did he say to you?" Jack wished he was there to put German in his place. He huffed. But then again, it was probably best he wasn't around.

Luke rolled his eyes and explained, "Just talking shit to get me riled up before the game, nothing I can't handle." He kissed Jack, pulling him close and into a tight hold. "I just need a few kisses and I think I'll be able to beat him tonight." He let his lips trace down Jack's chin to his neck, making him shy away.

"Oh god, could you two not," Gabe whined. "I think you've been motivated enough." He watched as the two continued to hold each other, sharing a few more kisses before letting go. Jack took Luke's hand and they headed outside. "First you make out in front of me and then you leave me," Gabe complained, jogging behind them.

"We're gonna go get pizza before Luke has to get ready," Jack replied. He jumped as Gabe slapped his arm across his shoulders, squeezing between him and Luke.

"Oh, then I'm definitely not missing out!"

Jack pushed the gym doors open and shook his head.

"How do you expect to date anyone if you can't even give a girl a call or text back the next morning?" he questioned, glancing back at Gabe.

The other shrugged, following him up the bleachers and replied, "I usually don't get their numbers." Jack scoffed and took a seat.

Luke looked into the crowd and smiled when he saw Gabe and Jack. He sat down at his bench and his team watched as Middleton walked in. He could see a smirk on German's face, but he looked away. The matches began, teammates competing one by one. When it was finally his turn, he stood and walked onto the strip.

"Looks like you're well acquainted with Jack," German suddenly said to him.

"And if I am?" he responded. He put on his mask and they bowed at each other.

"Word of advice don't bother with him. All he wants is your money." Luke scoffed and waited for the referee's call.

Jack anxiously watched as his ex and current went head-to-head. All he could do was hope that asshole wasn't messing with wasn't messing with Luke's head. Luke was a few points away from winning the match, but German began catching up. He moved forward with his foil and Luke moved back, striking for the final score. Jack stood in excitement and clapped, Gabe joining him. Luke smiled up at him, taking off his mask, but his lips soon curled down when he heard the words that came out of German's mouth.

"How much did you pay him before he let you fuck him?" Luke turned to him and chuckled.

"What did you say?"

German got closer and responded, "He clearly looks like a fucking pet. Clapping up there like a happy dog." Luke could hear his coach telling him to break it up, but it was already too late. "I bet it's one sweet fucking ass." Luke smirked and he grabbed German, head butting him.

"Shit," Jack exclaimed. He tried rushing down the bleachers and over to Luke and German. Luke punched German in the face and the other fell to the floor. He got up but before he could get even one swing in, Luke was back on him. He punched German again, ripping the skin on his lip. The other tried shoving him off and managed to kick him in the chest. He went for a swing when his coach pulled him back.

"This game is over, Tom," the Middleton coach declared. "Your boys are out of control."

"Well, tell your fucking boy not to talk about my boyfriend like he's a fucking piece of meat."

German laughed and replied, "Oh, how I wish I had a taste." Luke went to hit German again, but his teammates were holding him back.

The referee turned to the audience and said, "Due to the insubordination of a Thomas Pry teammate, they have been disqualified."

"What happened today is never acceptable," Mr. Finnegan said. Luke, along with German, were sitting in the vice principal's office. "Now, do you boys want to tell me what started this altercation?"

"Go on, tell your daddy what happened?" German taunted. Luke stood and walked to the back of the office. If he sat next to him any longer, he would kill him.

"Mr. Williams," Mr. Finnegan said sternly. "I will not tolerate that type of insolence in my office, let alone at my school."

German huffed and looked away. "I'm sorry."

Mr. Finnegan sat back and ordered, "Tell me what happened."

German scoffed and answered, "I said one thing about his boyfriend, and he went completely berserk on me."

"You called Jack a dog. And you tried to tell me that he's only with me for my money!" Luke protested.

"Mr. Finnegan," Luke looked at his dad and huffed, folding his arms. "Now, I find this argument to be quite childish and unnecessary. Mr. Finnegan, it was very inappropriate of you to put your hands on Mr. Williams."

"What? He—"

"However, Mr. Williams, you should not be speaking of Mr. Whyte. If I am not mistaken, you two had an altercation at Middleton which resulted in his expulsion and transfer to this school. Which indicates to me that you should not be discussing him with anyone." Mr. Finnegan huffed, and he looked between the boys. "Thomas Pry and Middleton will take disciplinary actions for your behavior today. Mr. Williams, please stay seated while I contact Middleton."

"Whatever." German grumbled, crossing his arms. Mr. Finnegan looked up at his son and nodded toward the door.

"You are excused for now." Luke nodded and walked out of the office.

Jack stood and looked at Luke.

"Hey," he muttered, taking the other's hand. Luke huffed and rested their foreheads together.

"I'm sorry for letting him get to me," he muttered. "He was just saying really shitty things and I couldn't let him go back without a few bruises." Jack managed a chuckle and held Luke's cheeks.

"It's alright. He definitely deserved it." Luke smiled and he kissed Jack.

"What do you think your dad will do?" Jack asked.

Luke shrugged and replied, "He'll probably tell Middleton about German and I fighting and then just leave it up to my coach to give me whatever penalty he sees fit." Jack nodded and sighed.

"His parents will make sure he doesn't get this put on his record, but at least I'm not the only one who knows how terrible he is now." Luke chuckled and kissed Jack again.

"Well, I guess he's got the money to keep your ass happy," German commented. Jack and Luke looked at each other before looking at him.

Jack went to say something when Mr. Finnegan came out of his office. "Mr. Williams, if I have to speak to you one more time, I will make sure you face heavier penalties at Middleton." German closed his eyes and huffed. "Now sit down and wait to be picked up." He gritted his teeth and plopped down into a chair. Mr. Finnegan looked at Luke and Jack and ordered, "Come in." Jack looked at Luke with confusion before following him.

"D-Did I do something?" he asked, watching Mr. Finnegan sit down. The man looked up at him and managed a smile, something Luke hadn't seen in a while.

"Not at all," he reassured. He gestured to the seats in front of him and the boys sat. Mr. Finnegan looked at his son. "What you did, while very inappropriate, took a lot of guts. You risked being kicked off the team for the person you care about and I am proud of you for that."

Luke gulped and replied, "Th-Thanks…Dad." Mr. Finnegan smiled again, and his eyes shifted to Jack.

"If for any reason, Mr. Williams harasses you again, let me know and I will take care of it."

Jack nodded and responded, "Okay. Thanks, Mr. Finnegan."

"Of course. You boys head home." They both nodded, said their last thank yous, and headed out the office door. They ignored German who glared at them and continued down the hall.

"Your dad is fucking awesome," Jack exclaimed, looking up at Luke. The other scoffed and shook his head.

"The last time he told me he was proud of me, I won my first match in my 11th year," he confessed.

"So what? He just told you he was proud of you for kicking German's ass. And he put German in his place." Luke tried to hide his smile, but it was too obvious.

"Yeah, I guess he did."

Luke brushed his hair back and sighed. He looked in the mirror, smiling. He couldn't wait to see Jack. He saw him wearing the suit when they were at the fitting but tonight would definitely feel different.

"Are you going to pick up Jack?" Luke turned around and smiled at his father, his mother at his side.

"Yeah," he replied. His mother walked up to him and ran her hand down his cheek, holding it.

"I hope you have an amazing time sweetheart," she exclaimed.

Luke nodded and replied, "Thanks, Mom. I hope he does too."

"I'm sure he will, son," his father said from the doorway. Luke nodded and they all made their way downstairs to the front door.

"You ready, kiddo?" Ralph called out from the limo.

"Yep!" Luke exclaimed and jogged to the car.

Jack paced back and forth. Although he was anticipating tonight, he was very nervous. He didn't really go to Middleton parties, and he definitely didn't dance. Jack kept walking back over to his mirror, checking his tie. His mother had tried to give him a superman curl, but it just didn't work. He pushed it out of his face and huffed.

"Hey, bud, ya feeling alright?" Jack turned and saw his father. He huffed with a small chuckle and smiled.

"Not really…" He looked around before looking at him again. "Dad, have you ever…had such deep feelings for someone that, whenever you're not around them, you can't stop thinking about them?"

Jack's dad smiled and asked, "Is that how you feel about Luke?"

Jack sat on the bed and mumbled, "Yeah."

His dad sat beside him and patted his leg, explaining, "Well, kiddo, when I was younger and I met your mom, I couldn't stop thinking about her. She was my everything and now that we're married, she is the number one thing on my mind. I guess what I'm trying to say is, when you love someone, there's not a moment you stop thinking about them because, well, they're your new world." Jack looked at his father before smiling and giving him a hug. They heard a horn honking and Jack sighed.

"That's Luke," he said. He let go of his father and stood.

Jack's father looked up at him and smiled. "Have fun, kiddo." Jack nodded before making his way downstairs. His mom slowly got up from the living room couch and walked over to him.

He kissed her on the cheek and smiled at her. "Later, Mom."

"Have fun, sweetie!" she shouted after him. Jack waved back at her, opening the door. He bumped into someone and looked up.

"I was going to ring the bell." Jack smiled and kissed his boyfriend.

"Sorry, Luke, I'm not used to this stuff."

Luke smiled and replied, "Sorry, babe, should've warned you then." He wrapped his arms around the other's waist and kissed him again. He looked over Jack's shoulder and waved at Jack's mom. "Goodbye, Ms. Whyte."

"Have fun, boys!" Luke smiled and pulled Jack out of the house.

"You ready for tonight?" Luke asked.

Jack sighed and confessed, "I'm still a little nervous."

"Don't worry, it's gonna be fun."

Gabe watched as a black limo pulled up in front of the school's lot. He could see Ralph in the driver's seat, and he waved at him. The man waved back and out stepped Luke and Jack, the two holding hands and walking toward him.

"Well, look who finally showed up," he exclaimed.

Luke asked, "Where's your date?" He pulled on the other's purple tie and chuckled.

Gabe glared at him before explaining, "I saw a lot of girls wearing purple so I'm gonna try my luck."

Jack patted the other's shoulder and replied, "Good luck."

Gabe rested his arm across Jack's shoulders and responded, "I love your sarcasm." The three walked into the building and were overwhelmed by the music. "Well, boys, have fun. I'm going to find me my lady." Gabe gave the couple a thumbs up before walking away.

Jack looked at Luke and he just smiled before pulling Jack into the crowd of dancing teenagers. "L-Luke, let's uh, get some drinks."

"What? You don't wanna dance?"

"Maybe later?" Luke pouted before holding the other's waist. Jack kissed him and Luke smiled.

"Alright, you win." He took the other's hand, and they walked over to the drinks.

"Luke, you're going to come dance with us, right?" a girl asked, standing beside Jack. The other looked at her with a raised brow and she smiled. "Don't worry, we won't steal him for long," she attempted to reassure. Jack turned to Luke and the other laughed.

"Sorry, I'm not getting on that dance floor until my boyfriend wants to." Jack looked back at the girl and smiled. She pouted and went to turn away when another teen spoke.

"You can dance with me." It was Gabe and he was reaching over to grab the punch bowl spoon from Jack's hand.

"Why would I want to dance with you, Gabe?" Before he could even respond, she walked off. Gabe turned to his friends who were clearly trying to hold back their laughter.

"What's so funny, huh? I won't find a date if I don't try my luck." Jack rolled his eyes and grabbed Luke's hand, pulling him along.

Luke watched and followed as he was squeezed between people. When they finally stopped, he wrapped his arms around Jack from behind. "Looks like someone changed their mind," he said in the other's ear.

Jack shrugged. "Might as well before every girl and possibly guy starts asking for a dance." Luke chuckled and rested his chin on the other's shoulder.

"I would reject them all in a heartbeat." Jack smiled and turned to give his boyfriend a kiss. Their bodies began moving to the smooth salsa music that blasted throughout the room. Jack bit his lip as he felt the other's hands moving down his waist.

"Hey!" They jumped as they heard a faculty member shout. "You two are already on thin ice after that kiss," they warned. Luke's eyes went wide and he waved at the faculty member.

"Sorry." Jack shook his head, raising his cup of punch to his lips. "Guess this is as close as we can get," Luke moped. Jack smiled and pinched his cheek.

"We can always…disappear for a few minutes," he suggested, letting his eyes roam.

"Forget a few minutes. Should we leave right now?" Luke teased, leaning in close to the other's ear. "Should I call Ralph?"

"I won't tell you two again!" The couple began laughing and they stepped back from one another.

"I think we should enjoy prom," Jack declared, smiling. "Let's drive faculty crazy a little longer." Luke smiled and nodded.

"Agreed."

After some more attempts to get closer and a lot of shouting over the music, Luke and Jack had taken off their suit jackets, Luke removing his tie at some point in the night.

"Has Trish ever had the luxury of dancing with you like this?" Jack asked, resting his head on Luke's shoulder and wrapping his arms around his neck. It was time to slow dance-the only dance they would be able to embrace each other without getting yelled at.

"Yeah, once or twice," Luke muttered. "Why, you jealous?"

"Why would I be?" Jack smirked and looked up at the other. "You're my boyfriend now. Or have I been reading this all wrong?"

Luke chuckled. "No, you haven't. I'm your boyfriend and you're mine." The two swayed from side to side and as the lights dimmed, Luke took this as an opportunity. He leaned down and kissed Jack's shoulder, then his neck, and then his cheek. Jack looked at his boyfriend and kissed him. Before they could exchange any other words, the DJ had an announcement to make. He stopped the music, and everyone turned to him.

"Alright, kids, it's time to announce prom king and queen." Someone handed him a paper and he opened it. "Your prom King and Queen are Luke Finnegan and Kathy Hogens." Luke kissed Jack before walking up onto the stage. Jack stood and watched as Luke danced with the girl before taking a seat.

"Well, would you look at that." Jack smirked and turned his head to Gabe. "You wanna go break them up? I'll grab her, you grab him?" Jack chuckled and shook his head.

"I'm all good. Did you find anyone?" Gabe pouted and shook his head before gulping down his drink.

"I almost flirted with Trish." He shivered. "If she hadn't turned around so quickly, I would have had a mountain of troubles." Jack chuckled and patted the other's shoulder.

"You did say any girl in purple." Gabe gawked at him and Jack couldn't help but laugh.

"You're the worst you know that?" Gabe huffed before sitting up straight. "Well while it wasn't my lucky night, there's always university!" Jack nodded, smiling at his friend. But why did he suddenly feel uneasy from the last word he spoke?

"We hope you all had a great night, Thomas Pry!" the DJ shouted, and everyone cheered. Jack looked up and watched Luke jog over to him.

"Let's go," he said, reaching out his hand. Gabe and Jack looked up at him in confusion and he smiled.

"You don't wanna stay longer?" Jack asked.

Luke shook his head, took his hand, and replied, "I've got a surprise for you."

"Okay," Jack stretched. He looked at Gabe and the other put his thumbs up. He stood and Luke pulled him along.

"Are you gonna tell me where we're going or am I gonna have to guess?"

Luke, pushing the school doors open, shrugged and answered, "You'll find out when we get in the car." He looked around and saw the limo parked at the furthest end of the school's main building. When they reached it, they got in and Luke handed Jack his tie. "Put this around your eyes."

Jack furrowed his brows and questioned, "Where the hell are we going?"

Ralph chuckled. "Have you not told him?"

"It's supposed to be a surprise," Luke whined. "C'mon." Jack hesitated, staring at the tie. Luke wouldn't try to kidnap him, right? He took the tie and put it around his eyes, making a knot in the back of his head. "You can't see me, right?"

"Barely."

"Okay good, let's go, Ralph."

"Yes, sir."

Luke looked at the terrified Jack and kissed him on the cheek. "You're gonna love it, I swear." The rest of the ride was quiet, but a million and one questions ran through Jack's mind.

"Alright, boys, call me when you're ready to be picked up," Ralph ordered. Luke nodded and he looked at Jack.

"Alright, grab my hand."

"I don't understand why I have to be blindfolded," Jack complained, reaching out for Luke's hand. The other caught it and helped him out the car. He walked around the vehicle as it went to pull off and continued onto the grass. Jack could feel the crunch under his feet, and he moved closer to

Luke. "I know you probably won't tell me but am I about to be murdered?" Luke laughed and shook his head.

"No, we're on a pretty beautiful hill," he said.

"Well," Jack replied, putting his hands to his face to pull off the tie. "Can I at least..." He had to be dreaming. "Where the hell are we?" They stood on a hill, just like Luke said, but the view was so much more than Jack could've imagined. In the distance was a forest, the branches highlighted by the stars and moon that painted the sky. Right below the trees was a lake, filled with the calls of frogs and the tiny lights of fireflies. "Is this real?" he asked, looking at Luke. The other took a seat and nodded.

"My parents own this. It's part of their estate they bought together when they first got married," he clarified. Jack stared at the beauty in front of him and did his best to sit down without turning his head.

"It's fucking amazing," he breathed. He looked at Luke and pulled him into a kiss. The other smiled and gently pulled away. He huffed and rested his elbows against his knees, his hands over his mouth. Luke took a deep breath before finding his words.

"I know we're probably not going to the same university, considering you're studying architecture and engineering and I'm doing law." He sighed and looked away. "But I want us to do our best to keep seeing each other...I uh, I don't want to lose you."

Jack smiled and reached over, grabbing Luke's hand. "Of course, Luke. I won't be too far so we can hang out on the weekends. And we still have the summer."

Luke nodded and he huffed, "You're right...I don't know. I guess I just got a little freaked." Now he turned to

Jack. "I guess what I'm trying to say is that I really like you…I like you and I wanna spend a lot more years with you."

Jack scoffed and kissed Luke. "I like you a lot too and I'm happy to be your boyfriend." Luke smiled and tackled Jack.

"When did you start saying such cheesy things?"

Jack laughed. "Ever since I started dating you." He sighed and stared at Luke before closing his eyes, and letting Luke kiss him. When they parted, they smiled at each other before dedicating their attention back to the nature that danced in front of them.